Die This Day

When their troubled town found itself yet again without a peace officer to enforce the law, the citizens finally agreed on what must be done: forget the cost and risks involved and hire a town-tamer.

The famed marshal seemed to meet all their requirements – until the day gun hell erupted again.

The town looked confidently to their hero to deal with the trouble – while only the marshal himself realized that this town – and this adversary – might prove the one to put him in his grave.

By the same author

Shannon
Five Guns from Diablo
Badlands in My Blood
The Last Hero
A Town Called Limbo
Too Fast to Die
Just Breathin' Hate

Die This Day

Dempsey Clay

ROBERT HALE · LONDON

First published in Great Britain 2009

ISBN 978-0-7090-8705-2

Robert Hale Limited
Clerkenwell House
Clerkenwell Green
London EC1R 0HT

www.halebooks.com

Typeset by
Derek Doyle & Associates, Shaw Heath
Printed and bound in Great Britain by
CPI Antony Rowe, Chippenham, Wiltshire

CHAPTER 1

THE TOWN-TAMER

A gust of rain-laden wind followed Marshal Cord Ashton as he shouldered his way through the batwings into the saloon.

Dirty weather had been threatening for days and now it had finally come with heavy raindrops pounding into the deep dust along the broad length of Elm Street in the town called Pepperbox.

The Paradise Saloon was a sprawling, comfortable establishment that catered to the town's businessmen and the well-heeled, leaving the Red Dog and Lucky Nugget to the cowboys and citizens with a taste for cheap whiskey and rough company. That night, due to the turbulent weather, there were few customers in the place when the lawman brought that cold wind eddying in behind him before the batwings flapped shut.

All heads turned as Ashton came to a halt just inside to look about him.

In his tenure here the marshal had put his stamp on Pepperbox with greater impact than any man in the town's history. The council had hired him at one hundred dollars a week in desperation when the excesses of brawling miners, wild cowboys and drunken drifters had failed to respond to a succession of peace officers, some of whom had lasted less than one full week at the job.

Yet during his months in office the only citizen to be buried in Pepperbox had been the widow Jackson, taken off by the colic in her eighty-third year. Cord Ashton had put the lid on troubled Pepperbox with gun, fists and an iron authority, then nailed it down tight without having had to shoot anybody down in the process.

'Ahh, Marshal Ashton,' greeted Mayor Sam Ridge, making an expansive gesture from his chair at the poker layout. 'Come join us, man. Bo, make a place for the marshal.'

Moving deeper into the saloon and removing his low-crowned grey Stetson, Ashton made to shake his head. He didn't care for gambling and had little taste for idleness. Yet then he changed his mind, suddenly aware there was a limit to just how many ways a peace officer could occupy his time fully in a town which now appeared thoroughly tamed.

'Some night, eh, Marshal?' grinned storekeeper Denton as the lawman exchanged nods with the players. Denton, a lean and raw-boned man, carried his empty left sleeve pinned across his shirtfront. A drunk's bullet had cost him the limb several months back, but there had not been a single shot fired within one hundred yards of the central block since Ashton had taken over.

'Some night indeed,' Ashton agreed in his formal way, instinctively passing up the first chair offered to move around the table where he finally sat with his back against a solid wall. 'Table stakes?'

'Table stakes, Marshal,' affirmed dealer Chips Garland, and the cards went around and around.

The lawman provided a strong contrast in appearance to the others gathered about the poker layout as the first hand was decided, and Garland dealt again. Just thirty years of age, Ashton appeared older due to his serious manner and the weight of responsibility he'd carried through five years spent behind a marshal's star in a succession of places just like Pepperbox.

Tonight as usual he was dressed conservatively in dark suit and riding boots with a black tie against a pale blue shirt. His face was long-boned and deeply bronzed by the western sun. He had a way of carrying himself that was halfway between confident and arrogant. He was a man who seldom really relaxed, whether he be in the company of friends, as now, or out upon the dangerous streets going against those who would hold law and order to ransom.

'Bettin' or passin', Marshal?' asked Sam Ridge, as

money hit the centre.

Ashton realized he wasn't concentrating. He glanced absently at his hand. 'Pass.'

'You was a long ways away just then, Marshal,' Ridge smiled. 'Something on your mind?'

'Perhaps, Mayor,' Ashton replied in a way that discouraged further probing.

Leaning back he turned down his cards and reflected upon the letter tucked away in the inside pocket of his broadcloth coat. He'd received it just that morning from Sugar Creek, begging him to return there and take up the position of town sheriff, the former position he'd relinquished a full year ago now. He'd quit his posting there for reasons known only to himself. But now with yet again another peace officer gunned down upon the streets out there it seemed plain Sugar Creek had slipped back into the bad old days of gun law.

Normally a man of quick and firm decisions, Ashton had uncharacteristically mulled over this request throughout the day. He was still indecisive some twenty minutes later when the batwings screeched open and trouble came jingling in on big rowel spurs.

The only player uninvolved with the game at the moment, the lawman gave the young stranger with the wild thatch of red hair little more than a cursory glance. At first. Then, ever so briefly, as the man stood there allowing his eyes to accustom to the lights, he permitted his gaze to stray momentarily and meet the newcomer's.

Even at thirty feet distant through smoke-filled air Ashton felt that cold green-eyed stare almost like a physical push before the stranger turned away to make his supple-hipped way across to the long bar.

That brief glance was enough for the marshal – and more than enough to alert those keen instincts without which the town-tamer might never have survived the past years to be sitting here virtually unscathed amongst the good citizens of Pepperbox.

'I will buy two cards, Mr Garland,' he murmured quietly, as the stranger ordered whiskey.

Nat York, the gunsmith, bet a dollar, Ridge bumped him two and Ashton paid to see.

He glanced up again.

The newcomer now stood staring at him directly with his whiskey glass held in his left hand.

The instant he saw this the lawman's stare cut narrow and cold.

For no matter what the circumstances, any man who lived by the gun – such as himself – always kept his right hand free. This was just one of many laws of survival Ashton and his fast-gun breed lived by. And his next probing stare warned him that the cold-eyed youth with the bright red hair sticking out from beneath his hat had guntipper stamped all over him.

He surveyed the smoke-filled room to see if anyone else was aware of the new arrival. Plainly none was. These were towners here, comfortable and peaceable men in the main, who mostly only ever worried about profit and loss – not about wild boys who might show up out of noplace looking to raise hell.

But was this one really doing that?

Ashton could not be sure for the breed could be as unpredictable as it was dangerous.

But when he caught another flinty-eyed stare from across the room, uncertainty vanished and suddenly anger knotted his guts. He'd been down this street too often before to be mistaken! This one was trouble with a capital T. That breed came after names, they sought you out and they could make it impossible for you not to respond to a challenge. . . .

At moments like this he hated this kind worst of all, for they were men prepared to take a life or lose their own for no logical reason.

'Marshal,' Sam Ridge chuckled, drawing his attention back to the table. 'I'm afraid you're wool-gathering again.' He winked at his companions. 'You know, if I didn't know the marshal better I'd almost reckon he had a woman on his mind, eh, boys?'

This was only spoken in jest yet mere minutes earlier it would have been right on the mark. For a woman had totally dominated Ashton's thoughts ever since that letter from Sugar Creek. He supposed he had this blow-in to thank for dragging his full attention back to the here and now.

The stranger suddenly started towards the poker layout with a purposeful step and Ashton was dangerously alert by the time he propped just a few feet away, to remark, 'You just gotta be that hotshot marshal these folks simply won't hesh up about, right?'

The room hushed and the game stopped dead. Every eye at the table swivelled around to the source of the mocking remark. They took in the youngster with the tied-down cutter and old Sam Ridge gasped aloud, reading his brand only too clearly.

Only Ashton appeared calm as he eased his chair back a little from the table.

He didn't speak; you could always rely on this breed to do all the jawing. They couldn't help themselves. They had to gear themselves up before challenging a man – and maybe getting themselves killed. How he loathed the breed! And he was tempted, if only for the moment, to draw and blast the ugly little bastard out of his fancy boots without warning – as he likely deserved.

But he didn't, and his adversary read his reluctance as weakness.

'I am Lee Jenner from Daybreak County,' he announced, right hand hanging close to the handle of a rusty old Colt. 'You jugged a pal of mine recent, Ashton, then got him sent up to County Jail for six years' hard. Remember Tommy Walsh?'

Ashton rose unhurriedly but the gun kid jumped back in alarm. Someone sniggered and his face turned choleric with anger and embarrassment. 'Not another step, lawdog!' he warned. 'One more move and I'll let you have it, swear to God!'

Ashton kept coming around the big circular table. This scene was as old as the first day he'd pinned on a star. Its key elements were the wild kid hunting gun glory, a hushed and expectant audience, the prospect of death and gunsmoke thick in the air. The only uncertain factor, as was eternally the case, was the outcome.

'I warned you, tinstar!' the kid hollered as customers went diving for cover and a percenter screamed shrilly. 'So you better back up!'

'Why, son? To give you time so's you can screw up your nerve?' Cord's voice was a lash. 'I know your breed, kid. You want to kill a man just so you can boast about it to your friends. But you are not cut out for this game and never will be. I've faced a hundred like you and you're all nothing. I was better with a gun wearing diapers than you are today – you stink with mediocrity!'

His purpose was to fluster and confuse the punk long enough to reach him. He almost made it. The redhead began trembling with his eyes rolling in their sockets. He tried to curse but his mouth was too dry. He darted a wide-eyed look back at the batwings, and Cord kept his fingers crossed that he just might prove to be smart enough to cut and run.

But he wasn't. Something – either fear or pride – caused him to shake and dribble out a garbled curse, then launch into the draw.

Ashton had closed the gap to a bare few feet when he made his play – and knew he was now close enough. Moving faster than seemed possible he lunged forward at the same time whipping out his Colt to chop viciously down upon Jenner's gun arm before his weapon could clear leather.

The unfired piece clattered to the floor and the marshal's momentum kept him driving forwards to pack everything behind a right to the jaw that belted the man backwards to smash against the bar then crumple face downwards to the floor, out cold and bleeding from the mouth.

Ashton allowed his momentum to carry him on towards the batwings and away from the sudden shocked silence behind. As he approached the batwings a citizen jumped from his path, fearful of the expression on the lawman's face.

It was this look that halted Ashton from going through the doors and out into the night. For he didn't want honest men afraid of him; that wasn't what the badge on his vest was for.

He propped, sucked his knuckles then brushed back an errant strand of hair before turning to face a hushed room.

'Doc,' he called to fat old Doc Bindale, seated pop-eyed close by in a corner. 'C'mon, I'll tote him up to your place.'

'S-sure, whatever you say, Marshal,' Bindale replied, and a wave of relief washed through the saloon as Ashton threw the unconscious kid over one shoulder to follow the medico on out through the batwings into the rain.

All anger had abated before he'd gone ten yards with his burden, his anger immediately replaced by something entirely different.

Gratitude.

For the kid's attack had suddenly made him realize clearly that his job in this man's town had been accomplished. For how long was it since there'd been any real trouble here? Too long had to be the answer. And when a town tamer with empty cells found himself mostly tangling with proddy kids and drunks instead of killers and cow thieves, it meant only one thing.

Time to move on.

One thing no top badgeman was never short of on the frontier, was towns in trouble. Already he knew what he would do and where he would go.

With his busted arm in splints and heavy strapping around his head, Lee Jenner was a sorry sight as he struggled to sit erect in his saddle. Yet ride he would, because the sheriff said he must.

'You mightn't realize it just yet but you're a mighty lucky kid,' Ashton assured. 'You're as slow with a Colt as a fly in molasses and nine out of ten kids I know here could beat you to the draw and shoot blindfold. So get back home, get yourself a steady girl and a job – and think yourself lucky. Like . . . real lucky.'

With the words, Ashton brought the flat of his hand down on the horse's hindquarters and the kid was riding off into the misting night, hurting, humiliated – yet alive.

'Reckon he'll make it home and take your advice, Marshal?' Sam Ridge queried as they watched the swaying figure swallowed by the darkness beyond the frail rim of the town lights. 'Not that anybody would give much of a damn though, I guess.'

'He'll make it home,' Doc Bindale declared, hopping back in beneath the awning, 'on account he's scared silly and is smart enough to realize how lucky he is. Well, I've said it before and I'll say it again, Marshal, what would we do without you in Pepperpox?'

'Good question, Doc,' Ashton said soberly. 'And one we are going to discuss over at the Council Chambers, right now – tonight!'

The bystanders thought this sounded ominous. And it was.

It didn't take long to convince the council he was serious about quitting, yet some were still in shock as the mayor's wife appeared from in back with a tray laden with coffee.

So he took the time to explain.

'It's pretty simple, gentlemen. You see, I attracted that hot-head here tonight just the way I did that fool Strat Murray six weeks back. Neither of them would have had any interest in this town but for me and my reputation. It's happened to me before and I guess it will always happen. You can clean up a town, subdue the lawless elements and set it on the right track. But always when you have a gunfighter wearing a star you will have the young and hot-headed show up out of the tall grass to challenge you, and I don't have to tell you that sort of thing retards any town's civilizing progress and can end up giving it a bad name.'

His audience exchanged sombre glances but only Ridge still tried to protest.

'But, Marshal, surely you—'

'No!' Ashton overrode him. 'I have made up my mind, Mayor. I've outlived my usefulness here and I'm moving on. That's the end to it.'

Buck Stuart, the rugged young deputy Ashton had recruited and trained with this day in mind, appeared both glum and sober as he set his coffee mug upon the spur-scarred desk in the jailhouse's front office.

'Well . . . if your mind is all made up like you say, Marshal . . . where might you be heading?'

'Sugar Creek.'

Both men stared. Everybody knew Ashton had done a stint as town sheriff in wild Sugar Creek a year earlier, just as they were aware what a fine job he'd done in bringing the wild elements to heel out there. But tamed towns did not necessarily remain that way, and Sugar Creek had again become notorious of late with violence and killings frequently grabbing headlines.

'You've been approached, Marshal?' Ridge wanted to know.

'Correct.'

A silence ensued. At last Ridge sighed. 'Well, I can see you've made up your mind. . . .' He hesitated, then went on. 'Mind if I ask you something, Marshal? About Sugar Creek, that is?'

'Ask away.'

'Well . . . well I hope you don't take offence, but back when we were making up our minds to offer you a posting here we heard rumours that you'd left Sugar Creek while your job there was . . . still, well—'

'Unfinished?' Ashton concluded for him. 'Well, Mayor, I hate to admit that what you heard was correct, for Sugar Creek was a long way from being a tamed town when I up and quit.'

He paused, features shadowing. He stared out the open door at rain weeping across the street lights. 'I should have seen it through. . . .'

The mayor found this hard to swallow. Leaning forward in his chair, Sam Ridge said, 'This sure don't sound like you, Marshal.'

'Maybe that's why I'm going back now,' Cord said, moving to a window. 'I'd never left a job of work unfinished before.'

'You just said a "maybe", Marshal,' Ridge said, also rising. 'You don't sound too sure.'

'I will be,' Ashton predicted and picked up his hat from the desk, signalling that the parley was ended.

Yet his uncertainty was still evident an hour later as he was moving about his room at the Pepperbox Hotel, packing up his gear. For he couldn't be sure whether he was going back to Sugar Creek now because the wild men had taken over again since Sheriff Barney Tobin had been shot, or for a totally different reason.

The reality was that he knew he was desperately needed down there to reclaim order. That was normally all the reason he'd require to accept a contract and show up with badge and gun. But then, there was little that had ever been normal about that turbulent town.

Ashton crossed the room to open the French windows and step out on to the balcony in shirt-sleeves. A cold gust of wind pushed against him as he moved to the railing and stood motionless staring north . . . north in the direction of Sugar Creek.

'Barbara. . . .'

He spoke the name aloud and his hand went instinctively to the heavy gold watch chain slung across his vest. He drew the piece from his vest pocket, clicked it open and read the inscription engraved inside the lid. It read simply, 'To Cord from Barbara, 5 August, 1871'.

The watch closed with a click and slid back into his vest pocket as his thoughts drifted back to the day when Stirling Kincaid's sister had given him the gift. How often during that intervening year had he wondered, as he did now, whether she'd sensed the real reason he'd quit there, with his job still unfinished.

Had she suspected he'd left because he feared he

was falling in love with her, while knowing that love and marriage could have no place in the life of any man whose life was on the line every day he walked the mean streets?

He shook his head. Of course she would not have figured that! For Barbara Kincaid had known him as a friend, nothing more. He was the fool who'd fallen in love, not her. . . .

And that raised the big question. Why in hell was he going back now?

His steps were heavy as he went back to the room. He stared at the faded flowered wallpaper and the cracked and broken shade that covered the single high narrow window with its dingy curtains.

At the head of the bed upon one of the big brass posts hung his gunrig, the butt of the heavy Colt .44 thrusting out aggressively. The bureau, gloomy and impersonal; the washstand scarred by countless cigarettes; the worn linoleum and the lamp with the badly dented shade.

How many towns like Pepperbox had there been, and how many lonely nights had his door closed against the danger and uncertainty, leaving the man they called the town-tamer all alone – maybe even lonely.

Ashton shook his head violently to clear it. The very suspicion that he could actually be lonely or might yearn for something beyond the dangerous life and a dingy hotel room with faded flowered wallpaper peeling from the walls, was something he could well do without at that moment.

For a long space the man some claimed to have no weaknesses appeared transfixed by an invisible shaft of weakness impaling him.

Abruptly he shook himself and ran fingers through his hair, the haunted look was banished and he was soon once more himself, whole and strong.

He knew what he must do.

There was brisk purpose in his every movement as he crossed to the bed, pulled out his gun and sat down to clean it the way he did every night of his life.

He was going back to Sugar Creek because he was needed there, he told himself. No other reason. He would go with badge and gun and do whatever must be done to return it to what it had almost been when he'd left.

At last everything was clear in his mind.

Yet if this was so, why was it that he lay awake sleepless all night staring at the dancing lights reflected upon his ceiling from the rain-drenched street below, while listening to the tiny clicking of the watch on the small table at his bedside?

CHAPTER 2

RETURN OF THE TOWN-TAMER

Because Powder River was flooded they were forced to float the coach across, with the result that the stage was two hours late arriving at Sugar Creek on that cold wet night two days later.

Checking his watch as the dim lights showed up ahead, Ashton saw it was after midnight. He glanced across at the only other passenger and the big horse-breaker with the broken nose quickly looked away. The man had been full of whiskey and conversation when he boarded at Rawhide, yet had clammed up tight when Ashton deliberately revealed who he was and why he was going to Sugar Creek.

He knew the breed and understood how they thought.

They despised the man who wore the badge, or affected to, yet when things went wrong they were always the first to come running for the protection of the law.

That was just one of the many unpleasant facets of human nature he'd grown familiar with that no longer bothered him. Any more than he was concerned by the dull ache of the old bullet wound beneath his left shoulder blade which always acted up on chill and rainy nights like this.

'Sugar Creek comin' up!' the driver bawled down from his high seat.

Peering through the blurred mica windows of the stage, Ashton watched the first houses blur past and felt the old familiar hardness beginning to build inside, realized he'd had just two days' relaxation between duty in one tough town and another.

Was that enough?

It could never be enough.

The stage swung into Federation Street and he glimpsed the familiar façades of the general store; the Prairie Flower Saloon with its doors propped open in unspoken invitation to anybody still abroad and thirsty at this time of night; the barber shop; Chad Millen's Butcher and the Diamond Corral where he'd shot it out one night with Mad Billy Spring.

The stage depot loomed ahead, the broad-planked landing bathed in light. The coach rolled to a halt with the jingle of harness mixing with voices from the landing. The big wrangler picked up his battered bag as the stage door jerked open and the welcome clean smell of the rainy night cleared the stuffy coach interior. 'All out for Sugar Creek!' bawled the driver, loud enough to be heard a block away.

With a guarded glance at Ashton the wrangler stepped down first. Standing and stretching Ashton picked up his bag and followed, his movements stiff from long hours of sitting. With the stage running so late he did not expect to be met, yet stepping down, the first person he saw was Don Garrow, the mayor, and moments later in back of him, the grinning face of Lon Green.

'Marshal Ashton!' Garroway boomed. He was a tall and broad-shouldered man of fifty with a high colour and a bristling walrus moustache. He thrust out a big paw. 'Welcome back, Ashton, welcome back to our town!'

Shaking hands, Ashton murmured a response then turned as Lon Green approached.

'Howdy, Lon,' he said quietly.

'Good to see you, Cord.'

There was a vast difference between the two men's greetings and the overdone exuberance of the mayor. Cord respected Garroway, but Lon Green was one of the few men here he'd permitted himself actually to like.

Green was an orphaned young loner heading in the wrong direction when Ashton came to town, first to befriend him, then steer him in the right direction. An unlikely friendship had evolved yet one that had strengthened and survived nonetheless and it was a boost to find the man here to welcome him back.

'You've packed on some muscle, Lon,' he grinned, ignoring Garroway's obvious impatience. 'Keeping your nose clean, I hope?'

'Well, I ain't been riding horses into any saloons, if that's what you mean, Cord.'

Asthon's smile broadened. His introduction to the youngster had occurred when Lon had ridden a paint pony inside the Prairie Flower Saloon and the marshal had promptly tossed him into the hoosegow for his trouble.

'Glad to hear it, Lon,' he said, then turned back to Garroway. 'Too bad the stage was late, Mayor.'

'Yes, I understand, Ashton,' Garroway said, placing a hand on his shoulder. 'Now, if you'll excuse us Lon, Ashton and I have business matters to discuss.'

'Tonight?' Ashton queried, lifting his brows.

Garroway nodded and for the first time Cord realized the man appeared drawn and nervous.

'Tonight, even though I realize it's late and you must be weary.'

'That's all right.' He turned to the younger man. 'You compre how it is, Lon. We'll catch up tomorrow.'

'Sure, I'll be in town,' Green said in his easy way. 'Once again, it's sure mighty fine to see you back,' he added, and strolled off.

'I've booked you a room at the American House, Ashton,' Garroway informed as they started off down the street. 'Of course you can shift into the jailhouse later if you're of a mind, but just at the moment the law office is boarded up.'

'Since the sheriff was killed, you mean?'

'Keerect. Since Barney Tobin got it.'

With the stiffness and body kinks easing by this and the familiar plankwalks of Sugar Creek echoing beneath his boots, Cord angled his hat forward against the drizzling rain, marvelling at how swift was the transition he had made. Forty-eight hours back, Pepperbox had been his town and his responsibility. Now, one hundred miles from there, he was already shouldering the new troubles of Sugar Creek – the sort of troubles that could follow in the wake of a dead peace officer.

'Who killed Barney, Mayor?' he asked bluntly as they crossed Kiowa Street and passed under the shelter of the porch awnings again.

Kicking mud off his boots, Garroway raised a haggard face to the lights. 'It was McCrow from the Twenty Mile, Ashton. You didn't strike him before you left, did you?'

Ashton shook his head. He only knew McCrow by reputation but was all too familiar with the Twenty Mile cowboys, as wild a bunch of hellions who ever forked leather or shot up a town. Twenty Mile had given him plenty trouble back then before he'd whipped them into line. By the sound of things they had not stayed tamed very long.

'So, McCrow rides for Twenty Mile now?'

'As a troubleshooter,' the mayor's tone was thick with disgust. 'He's killed three men in the past three months – one of them the sheriff. But we'll go into that later if you don't mind. You see . . . well, there's something else. . . .'

Again the man's tension was obvious. Cord halted and looked him in the eye. 'Let me hear it.'

'Well . . . if you insist.' The man turned his back to the wind and said soberly, 'Stirling Kincaid is the concern right now.'

Ashton didn't change expression at mention of the boss of the huge Silver Dollar Ranch, a man whose arrogant ways had set him at odds with Cord the first day he'd come to Sugar Creek and who over time had virtually become an enemy.

'Trouble you say, Mayor?'

'Well, the truth of it is, what with things going so bad lately and Barney Tobin getting killed and all, well, in the end the council voted unanimously to send for you to ask you to come back and help us out. The only thing is we didn't tell Kincaid, mainly I guess because we didn't know how he'd take it . . . or how mad it might make him. . . .'

'I see.' He shrugged, hard-faced. 'Well, knowing this town and its long tongues I'd hazard he'd know about me by now.'

'Reckon so, and you can wager he'd be none too

happy. I don't have to tell you Stirling Kincaid can be one ornery sonofa when things don't go his way and—'

'So can I, Mayor Garroway,' he cut in. 'Now, if there's no more surprises, it's been a long day. I'll check myself in at the hotel. . . .'

'Let me show you there.'

'I know the way. I'll see you at nine in the morning at the jailhouse.'

'But, Ashton—'

That was all Cord heard as he stepped down into the street and headed for the American House Hotel. The rain was easing off at last and he could hear the sound of a piano drifting from the Hard Luck Saloon four doors along from the hotel.

It was strange how relaxed he felt as he checked himself in and climbed the stairs to his room, almost as if he had never been away. He was at ease at the moment and meant to stay that way. But, of course, that would depend a great deal upon Stirling Kincaid . . . and Barbara.

It was reassuring how peacefully he slept through his first night back in a very troubled town towards the end of winter. . . .

Next day broke fine and clear and the breakfast at the hotel was a good one. He was already accustoming to the curious stares and the occasional respectful nod, the whispering as he passed by.

'He really is back!' he heard a woman whisper, and

was encouraged to note she sounded relieved. Others he encountered as he entered the lobby didn't appear so relaxed. He could understand why. When he was here before, Sugar Creek was bordering on turning into a helltown with a Boot Hill far too large for a place its size. He'd whipped it into shape with dedication, hard work – and a ready Colt .45. Plainly, some folks remembered the gunplay more clearly than the peaceful law enforcement he'd presided over.

He shrugged. Town sheriff was no job for any man who expected to be liked or popular.

He paused in the lobby to remember what a fine place the American House always was. Solid, well-furnished and durable, it was all quality, nothing like the clapboard monstrosities they threw up in most towns like this one.

He turned and sighted Kincaid.

The rancher stood before the desk where a pale clerk was nervously polishing his spectacles. Feet wideplanted and with arms folded and head thrown back in the arrogant posture Ashton remembered all too clearly, the boss of Silver Dollar Ranch had obviously been waiting for him to appear.

The eyes that met the lawman's were chips of blue ice.

'So . . . you did come.'

Kincaid's voice was as deep and authoritative as he remembered. In the morning light of the lobby the lean face appeared flat and hard as though chipped from stone. Many unflattering things were said about Stirling Kincaid but none could deny he was a hard man with a formidable presence and uncompromising nature.

His own face blank, Ashton strolled across to the desk and dropped his satchel before turning to face Barbara Kincaid's brother.

'Why are you here?' The man's tone was cold and impersonal.

'You know damned well why, on account that weak-chinned Garroway has already told you.'

The desk clerk's eyes widened in alarm as Kincaid drew a step closer to Ashton. 'All right, if that's how you want to play it, Ashton. I'm here to tell you to your face that you're neither welcome nor needed back in this town.' A deliberate pause. 'I'm also here to say you won't be staying.'

'Is that a fact? Then that must mean that things have changed one hell of a lot since I was here last.'

'Meaning?'

'Well, back then you only ran the Silver Dollar, Kincaid. But you sound very much like you also run all Sugar Creek now. Would that be the case?'

Twin spots of colour showed high on Stirling Kincaid's cheekbones. Plainly stung by the other's sarcasm, he retorted, 'I always ran Sugar Creek, gunslinger, but that was something you never rightly understood.'

The man made an angry chopping gesture with his hand before continuing. 'Well, I'll make sure you understand me now. We don't want you here and never did for the very good reason your breed attracts far more trouble than you ever stop.'

'You're boring me for I've heard all this before from others just like yourself.' Ashton swung his back deliberately and spoke to the clerk. 'Here's my key.'

Stirling Kincaid's fists clenched at his sides, the colour draining from his face. Yet he managed to control his temper as the clerk scuttled for cover and Cord glanced back at him over one shoulder.

'All right, Ashton, let's stop beating around the bush. I want you gone for a dozen solid reasons, but I know it could take time to get what I want through the council. But there's one thing you won't test me out on, shooter, and that is the subject of my sister!'

Up until that moment the man had made little impression on Ashton apart from the obvious fact that his antagonism towards him had plainly deepened over time. Yet mention of Barbara caused a flicker of surprise to cross his face.

'Better make yourself plain,' Ashton said warningly.

'You know what I'm saying, you arrogant son of a bitch! Barbara is not for the likes of you and never was. No sister of mine is getting involved with any two-bit gunslinger hiding behind a badge . . . especially not for a second time. When she marries it will be to someone from her own class with whom she will in time produce heirs to the Silver Dollar Ranch. She is keeping company with Brett Cody at the moment and will continue doing so and you will stay away from her. You'll not speak to or have anything to do with her. You follow me – gunman?'

Finally stung, Cord retorted, 'Still fretting about the family lineage, Kincaid? And why is that, do you figure? Could it be that you've given up the idea of producing offspring yourself ever since your wife did the smart thing and left you?'

All colour drained from Stirling Kincaid's features. The man was shaking with the intensity of his rage. For an instant he appeared out of control, yet once again proved his self-mastery when he took three deeps breaths before responding.

'I could kill you for that, Ashton.'

'You mean have me killed, Kincaid. That's how you handle your dirty work that you don't have the ability or the guts for personally. But I walked into this town on my own two feet and that's how I'll leave when I've whipped it back into shape. I'll do whatever needs to be done here, however I see fit to do it. I'll go where I please and do whatever I want and if anybody doesn't like it then I won't be hard to find. That applies to any drunken bum who might take a shot at me on a dark night, and it sure applies to you!'

A silence fell as the two stood facing at close range, the hatred pulsing between them almost tangible. Then without another word Stirling Kincaid spun on his heel and strode out, tall in the doorway before he disappeared.

Ashton stood motionless for a full minute, then took out a cigarette and set it alight with steady fingers, drew deeply. It tasted just the way he was feeling, bitter yet strong.

He walked out to make his first daylight patrol of his town.

CHAPTER 3

THE VIOLENT STREET

The newly sworn-in sheriff of Sugar Creek quit the Prairie Flower Saloon and made his way along Federation Street. It was the following evening. The rain had blown away and the sun had shone throughout the afternoon yet the streets remained muddy, glistening now in the glow of the tallow lamps.

The boardwalks, three feet high in places, lined both sides of the street in the central block. Beneath them drunks and dogs slept while here and there a bewildered Indian squatted. Restless heels drummed above them night and day. There were cowhands abroad that day mixing with miners – blue-shirted and red-necked men, slow of foot, who contrasted sharply with the lithe, sun-browned men of the ranges who wore huge spurs which jingled musically upon the plankwalks.

His town – again.

A family passed Ashton by, the man in shiny store-bought clothes, the woman stolid and sturdy, leading children by the hand.

Many of those he encountered were newcomers attracted by the growing prosperity of Ramrod Valley, saloonkeepers, gamblers and lawyers in frock coats and bowler hats.

Here poverty and prosperity walked hand in hand, the backside out of denim trousers here, golden watch chains glinting in the sunlight there.

Ashton paused on the corner of Kiowa Street to light a cigar. His first full day was unfolding much more quietly than he'd expected. For after all this was no ordinary day. A lawman had been slain here and he'd come back to take over. Familiar faces he encountered showed uncertainty. He'd quit with a solid reputation yet they remembered he'd gone hurriedly for reasons most were unaware of. Since then trouble and violence had escalated in Sugar Creek. Big men were reaching out and grabbing with both hands, the undertakers were busy and he knew many of these folk who didn't quite meet his gaze were likely thinking, 'Might he quit on us again?' Or, more likely, 'Why did he leave like that before anyway?'

He didn't blame them. He'd left them vulnerable for grabbers and takers like Kincaid to take advantage of – now nobody seemed to know for sure what had brought him back.

He couldn't tell them. Or not yet, leastwise.

Sundown found him patrolling the seedy block two down from Main known as the Deadline, reflecting on his first day. There had been an altercation at the Hard Luck Saloon in the late afternoon but he had quelled it without finding it necessary to make any arrests. Apart from that incident Sugar Creek appeared to be on its best behaviour as he looked it over and was himself checked out in return.

Yet 'too quiet to last' remained his private assessment. He knew this town only too well.

Two blocks on from the Deadline he entered the slum sector known as Poortown. Whenever serious trouble erupted in Sugar Creek it often had its origin down here. But apart from one ruckus that might have had the potential for real trouble if he hadn't happened along when he did, peace prevailed.

The brawl that finally erupted was all over a can of peach juice. An out-of-work miner was seated on his own stoop sipping at his juice when the breed with a skinful showed up and claimed he'd stolen the stuff from his shanty, which was possibly the case.

The resulting fight was getting willing when Ashton appeared. Maybe he'd half forgotten that any man wearing a badge was the natural enemy along the Deadline, and next thing the combatants quitted belting one another and instead turned their venom on him with fists, boots and even the disputed tin can as weapons.

He put both on the pavement with just two cuts of a gunbarrel.

Even in that short space of time a mob had gathered, yet they fell back when he swung to face them with Colt still in hand.

'I'm walking soft here first day,' he advised quietly. 'But the next man to offend will dearly regret it. Better remember that.'

He turned his back and walked off and so instantly become the town's number one topic of interest. And over time the prime mystery surrounding him was, 'If Ashton was so eager to come back here, why in hell did he quit and leave us vulnerable the way he did before?'

It was a good question but nobody seemed to have the answer.

A quarter-hour later found him back on Federation Street making for the centre of town. As he passed the lighted windows of Toomey's Mercantile he nodded to a bunch of folks he'd never seen before but who plainly knew who and what he was.

And suddenly it all felt right, as he'd known it must with time. He was no longer the curiosity here but rather the hard-nosed lawman in a town that had been going to hell in a handcart.

It was a good feeling. He'd been under pressure last night and that feeling had been present in full measure this morning when he'd raised his right hand to swear the oath of office before Judge Niles and a full meeting of the Sugar Creek City Council in their chambers up on Main.

Now he felt on top of it all and knew the old feeling was back – that confidence that enabled him to walk streets like Federation with a badge on his vest as a potential target for any hellraiser who might drum up the nerve to challenge his authority, without a hint of unsureness.

And for a brief time at least, he didn't have to acknowledge the real reason that had brought him back.

'Coffee, Sheriff?'

He glanced up from his desk. The deputy was still nervous in his company, he realized. The man was only a couple of years younger but might have easily been twenty behind him in terms of experience.

He set his pen back in the desk rack and rose. 'Not now,' he said, reaching for his hat. He winked and added, 'Can I trust you to run things for an hour?'

'Reckon so, Sheriff Ashton,' the kid said brightly. He gestured towards the street. 'Everybody says you've got the wild ones so jittery they ain't likely to even spit on the sidewalks no more.'

'If that's so, Billy,' he said, going out, 'the one thing you can be certain sure of is that it won't last.'

Main Street was filled with sunlight.

His first stop on patrol was the Prairie Flower. He'd closed the place down before midnight last night due to noise and had been obliged to bang a couple of heads in the process. But no arrests. His first days were proceeding more smoothly than he'd expected and he was prepared to meet the troublemakers halfway by not coming down too hard, too soon.

The town's premier saloon was quiet at this time of day as he climbed to the second floor bar to peer in over the batwings. A dealer threw him a salute and a pair of desultory poker players glanced his way then began whispering between themselves. Cocking his head to the low murmur of voices, Ashton nodded in satisfaction and headed back downstairs. There was no suggestion of trouble at the Prairie Flower, or at least not this early – he was sure of that.

By this time he was growing used to the attention he attracted whenever he hit the street. There were naturally rumours circulating regarding why he'd seemingly left them in the lurch the last time, yet overall he felt he was welcomed by the majority and there was a general feeling of wary respect. He knew their curiosity would continue and the gossips would be asking one another, 'What's the true story about Sheriff Cord Ashton and Barbara Kincaid anyway?'

He could see the questions in their eyes but that didn't faze him. For his personal life would remain that way.

The stogie had gone out while he was making his way along the walk on his way back to the jailhouse. He stopped to relight when, from the far end of the street towards the Deadline, came the sound of two evenly spaced shots.

He nodded, sensed he'd been waiting for this. It

had had to come because Sugar Creek was that kind of a town, which was the reason he was here. Or at least one of the reasons.

He made off along Main and didn't slow until he sighted a freighter's wagon heading his way piled high with wet buffalo hides. Three riders rode escort, swaying in their saddles and singing, plainly drunk.

He paused on the edge of the walk. He didn't recognize the riders but there was no mistaking their horse brands. These men were off the Twenty Mile.

His frown deepened.

Unlike the powerful Silver Dollar Ranch which engulfed a third of Ramrod Valley, the Twenty Mile Ranch which lay that distance from Sugar Creek beyond the Rattlesnake Hills was a sprawling domain of stringy scrub cattle and wild men.

Hitch Judson was the owner who himself didn't know how many men he employed. What was well known, however, was that the Twenty Mile hands were the meanest bunch in the county and Ashton's former tenure in the sheriff's office had been highlighted by more than one set-to with the outfit.

'Hold!' he yelled, stepping down into the street as the cavalcade drew closer.

Horses were jerk-reined to a halt and three hard faces stared bleakly at the tall figure suddenly blocking their way. Two appeared impressed by the badge but the third, a high-shouldered ranny with a shiny head of curls so black they looked as if they'd been milled from coal tar, put on a sneer.

'Well, I be dogged if it ain't the new fire-eatin' sheriff!'

'Back up and shut up!' Ashton rapped, as citizens halted along the plankwalks to stare. 'I'm the new sheriff and I don't tolerate any kind of trouble including public drunkenness. Do I make myself clear?'

Two nodded in response but the man with the curly hair did not.

'Not all that clear, sir.' His tone was sarcastic. 'But what is clear from where I set is that you just gotta be this new wonder cowboy killer that's scaring honest folks out of their skivvies here of a sudden.'

Ashton's jaws tightened. 'What is your name, cowboy?'

'Curly Flynn!' the rider said with pride. 'Mebbe you heard of me. I'm Kell McCrow's saddle pard.'

It seemed to the onlookers that Ashton stiffened at mention of the name 'McCrow' – the Twenty Mile gunman who had shot down Sheriff Barney Tobin.

'I'll allow that does make a difference,' he said. 'Get off that horse!'

The hardcase paled, plainly taken aback. 'You got to be jokin'!' he retorted but got no further. For Ashton was moving forward – fast. His left hand reached up to seize Flynn by the waistcoat and one powerful jerk pulled him clear to hit ground hard. With a curse Flynn sprang erect only to be clipped across the forehead with a gun barrel. Instantly his body went flaccid and he fell back unconscious against his mount's forelegs, causing the animal to rear in alarm.

Federation Street seemed totally silent as Ashton shoved his six-shooter back into its holster.

'Pick him up!' he ordered. 'He is obstructing the traffic.'

Two waddies responded fast to heave the unconscious man across his saddle. They turned back apprehensively to face the lawman.

'When he comes round tell him he's barred from town for a month and that the next time he offends I'll see him packed off to County Jail.' He snapped his fingers. 'All right, move on. And remember my warning. No trouble!'

'Impressive, Sheriff Ashton . . . real impressive,' a mocking voice said loudly as the entourage moved off.

Ashton swung sharply to scan every face until the man who had called out chose to push his way through the crowd to face him squarely with right hand hooked in shell-belt and with fingertips touching holster.

'How do, Sheriff.'

The man was tall and moved with an easy grace. He wore striped pants and a white hat with a rattlesnake band around the rim. His face was lean and hard and though he was grinning now, that expression didn't touch bright black eyes. Around narrow hips hung a professional's gunrig, brass cartridges glinting in the light.

This was one of the fastest men with a six-shooter Sheriff Cord Ashton had ever encountered any place. Wild Jack Mason himself – gunfighter, gambler, killer.

'Mason,' Ashton murmured, turning to face him squarely. 'You looking to buy into trouble?'

The man smiled. 'Look for trouble with One-shot Ashton? You think a man is loco? You figure I wanna die?'

There was scorn and mockery in the man's tone but the sheriff let it pass.

'All right, Mason,' he said calmly. 'You and I are going to talk.'

It was a half-hour later, when coming along the jail-house porch Ashton paused at the sound of vigorous activity coming from the open doorway. He moved on to step inside and saw Deputy Lon Green sweeping his way through the archway leading into the cells.

'So,' he said, removing his hat and skimming it at the wall peg. 'What's all this?'

'Ah, it's you, Sheriff,' the youngster grinned, relief flooding his freckled face. 'You OK?' Raising a boot on to a stool then leaning his elbow upon his knee, Ashton appeared puzzled. 'Sure I'm all right, Lon. Why wouldn't I be?'

'Well, words gets around. I heard you'd tangled up with Mason. I was feeling so edgy I took to sweeping up. You sure everything's OK?'

'Sure.'

Ashton took out his chased silver cigar case and selected a golden stogie. 'Wild Jack and I just had a quiet confab over a glass of whiskey. We reached an agreement, much the same way as we did back in Boiling Fork. I agreed not to hound him providing he doesn't cause any trouble and he promised to play straight. So we shook on it. End of story.'

Lon Green heaved a sigh of relief yet continued to study the marshal intently.

'Sheriff, did you know Wild Jack was still in the region hereabouts when you elected to return to Sugar Creek?'

'No, I didn't. But it wouldn't have made any difference if I had.'

The deputy shook his head wonderingly. 'Tell me, Sheriff, you being real good with the guns and all . . . is that feller lightning like they claim? Everybody says he could carve a heap of notches on that gun of his if he was of a mind.'

Cord touched a match to his cigar and drew deep. He gazed out the window at the street, his gaze turning reflective now, thinking about Wild Jack.

'I saw him gunfight Morgan Dallas in Boiling Fork a year ago. Dallas fell dead with a bullet in his heart and with his gun still in his holster. I've not seen faster than that, for Morg was no slouch with the Colts.' He paused thoughtfully. 'Sure, Wild Jack is chain lightning with a gun. But I can tell you he's no fool either.'

Lon Green grinned proudly. 'Not fool enough to

brace you, eh, Sheriff?'

'Could be we both feel the same way about each other, Lon,' Ashton admitted. Then suddenly without warning he clapped both hands in front of his face then sent his right hand streaking for his gun.

Lon Green was laughing as he sent his own hand flashing down to gunbutt. This was a 'game' they'd played often before during idle moments in this very room during Ashton's first incarnation as sheriff of Sugar Creek when Green had been a wild kid he'd taken under his wing and taught him to look after himself and use a Colt.

Ashton came clear first now yet not by much. He smiled as he spun the weapon on his trigger finger and slipped it back into leather.

'You've been keeping up your practice I see, Lon.'

'Sure have, Cord.' The boy sighed. 'But you're still a country mile quicker, ain't you?'

'Don't ever get as fast as me,' Ashton said seriously now as he dropped his boot from the stool and moved behind the desk. 'For that is faster than any honest man ever needs to be and would only bring you trouble in the long run.'

Then, smiling again, he fished in his pocket and found a dollar bill. 'The heck with all that anyway. Here, go fetch some coffee from next door, and we'll kick back and talk a spell.'

The boy was back in minutes with two steaming mugs of hot and black from the eatery. With the pot-belly warming the room and the background murmur of town noises beyond the door, they settled down to talk. Leastwise, Lon Green talked, with Ashton prompting him occasionally and doing most of the listening.

First Lon revealed how he was making extra money roping and breaking wild horses in the Rattlesnake Hills. He then discussed matters concerning the town, filling Cord in on details of the worsening troubles with the Twenty Mile cowboys and the brawling gold miners who had only recently begun infesting the Rattlesnakes.

When he moved on to talk about Stirling Kincaid, then Barbara and Brett Cody, Ashton interrupted.

'And just how is Brett making out these days, Lon?' He sounded casual.

'Well, you know Brett. He still acts like he's worth a million when he mightn't have ten cents.'

Ashton nodded understandingly, reflecting on Brett Cody. Handsome, educated, athletic and with a fierce pride he'd inherited from his father, who had died several years back leaving his son boss of Bar 50 Ranch, young Cody had always been interested in Barbara Kincaid.

When Ashton quit Sugar Creek because of his own deepening interest in the same girl, he'd expected Barbara and Cody to wed, for she certainly deserved a man of his undoubted quality and standing.

Yet the couple had not married, and suddenly curious now, Cord asked the deputy the big question. Why not?

Lon Green considered a while before clearing his throat.

'Sorry, no real idea, Cord. I know Cody wants to get wed and it's no secret that Stirling wants them to get on with it.' He half-smiled. 'But I guess you know all about that?'

Lon was the only one Ashton had told of his clash with Stirling Kincaid at the American House the previous night. Cord nodded. 'Uh-huh, that's so. But if those two haven't become engaged yet, and both Stirling and Brett want it, then it must be Barbara that's delaying?'

'Well, you know her likely better than anyone, Cord. She's got a mind of her own. Oh, by the way, I saw her out by Silver Dollar this morning when I was taking a mule across to Seth Pickett's place. She was asking after you.'

Ashton felt his pulse pick up a beat. 'Oh?'

'Uh-huh. Asking quite a bit about you as a matter of fact. You know, how you are looking and suchlike. I told her you hadn't changed none.'

Cord's eyes smiled. 'And what is that supposed to mean?'

'Oh, you know . . . I just told her you was still as bossy and iron-mouthed as you were before.'

Ashton laughed and they lapsed into silence. It was comfortable silence with the feel of friendship in it which both allowed to drag on for some time.

Easy occasions like this were anything but commonplace for Cord Ashton, and the gunfighter wondered what it had been about the deputy kid that had enabled him to get close to him. Men of the gun could not really afford friends; it was like exposing a weakness that an enemy might capitalize on in a crisis. What he did know was that it was good to share a quiet hour with someone he genuinely trusted in his early time back in Sugar Creek.

The hour was drawing to a close. Ashton had just consulted his watch to see it had gone ten when the sound of running boots sounded on the plankwalk outside and moments later a pale-faced towner stood framed in the doorway.

'Sheriff Ashton!' he panted. 'There's a brawl broke out down at Kitty Dechine's Sporting House. Looks like a bad one!'

The raising of the alarm was warranted. It was surely a bad one which could have easily developed into something one hell of a lot worse, had not the marshal shown as swiftly as he did.

Ben Storch and Tinpot Tollver were roistering gold prospectors from the Rattlesnake Hills who'd somehow fallen out over the questionable favours of one of Kitty's tough girls.

The ladies were in the process of settling their differences with butcher's knives when Ashton came striding in.

He didn't hestitate. Two light taps from his six-gun barrel left the women conscious and mobile, but noisy no longer He'd seen one of them in action here a year before during which Kitty had been poleaxed by a heavy chair, and certainly the madam was in no way sorry to see them both led off tottering upstairs by her bouncers while she gratefully offered the lawman the hospitality of the house.

The offer was declined but Ashton did persuade Tough Kitty to close up for the rest of the day before he joined her in a mid-morning bracer of a cold beer followed by a small glass of her best rye, which was, as he'd remembered, damn fine sipping liquor.

All Sugar Creek was impressed by the sheriff's handling of a potentially bad situation at the bordello. Yet as he'd seen it do before both here and other places in the wake of trouble, Ashton in the course of the day noted a pronounced upsurge in minor dust-ups, the occasional brandishing of weapons and a general sense of disruption and petty crime . . . all triggered off by the ruckus at Tough Kitty's.

He dealt with it all by nightfall and the town seemed quieter despite a distinct feeling a big night was building up.

Ashton took an hour off to rest up at his hotel at dusk but dark-down found him on the streets again, refreshed and ready for whatever the night might throw up.

Yet by nine the whole place seemed to have quietened down and it might have been this that irritated the visiting boys from the Twenty Mile, prompting them to stage an impromptu horse race down

Federation Street which scattered men and riders left and right as they came thundering through, hooting and shooting at the moon.

The outward race was completed without incident but on their rip-roaring way back to the starting line they sighted the new sheriff standing in the centre of Federation Street with a Colt .45 in either hand.

He didn't yell or move as they came thundering towards him, and at the very last moment their nerve failed and the leading two horsemen first slowed, hesitated some more, then reefed their lathered mounts to a tail-sitting halt mere yards from the man with the gun.

Derisive cheering rose from the crowded sidewalks as, one after the other, in ones and twos, the rest of the street racers found a reason to quit until Kerrigan was the only one bent on staying the course, leaning low over his piebald's neck and plainly intending either to go through the sheriff or over him – whichever suited him.

The horse had more sense than the rider. It swerved at the last moment and as Kerrigan was flashing by the tall figure in the street, he emitted a triumphant yell that was cut brutally short when Ashton reached high and smashed him out of his saddle with a sweeping blow of gun barrel that dropped him unconscious in the horse's dust.

That put paid to the Great Horse Race but the night wasn't over yet. The seeds of rebellion had been sown and the ranks of the wild men were soon swollen by drunken towners, one of whom stopped off at the noisy Tinhorn Saloon an hour later to beat up on his girlfriend working there.

He was warming to his work when the sheriff came in, knocked him cold, then arrested him.

In the two hours following, special deputies were enlisted to jailhouse duty in order to process in turn Curly Flynn, offensive language, a drifter from across the border who, excited by the rebellious mood, saw fit to shoot out the street light in front of the bank. In all, seven troublemakers were cooled down then locked up before ten, at which time Kitty Dechine felt encouraged enough by what she had witnessed to reopen her place of business, despite advice to the contrary from various sources, including the new sheriff.

Turned out Kitty knew her town and her hellraisers best. The wild men had tested out the new lawman in town and absorbed the lesson he had handed out.

From the moment Kitty unlocked her doors until three in the morning when the last amiable drunk was put to bed, Sugar Creek enjoyed one of its quietest late evenings on record.

Back at the jailhouse for coffee in the small hours, Cord Ashton allowed the deputy to medicate a small scratch to the face and one skinned knuckle, comprising his only injuries.

The last deeply sobered roisterer had been released and the jailhouse was quiet with a cool wind blowing through the open windows by the time Ashton leaned back in his rocker and crossed his boots on the desk top.

This, he knew from long experience, was the night he'd had to have. He'd come to town without warning and the wild men had simply been waiting to test him out fully. They'd done so and he was well satisfied with the result. Of course, the outcome didn't mean that all the town's potential troubles were resolved.

Even so, he was well-pleased with the result later when he walked the empty streets of a sleeping town which just might have been put to the torch had the outcome been different.

It was with that solid feeling of satisfaction that he returned to his room at the American House, even if aware that, with Friday night out of the way, today was Saturday and Saturday nights could often be the worst.

He left instructions with the clerk to call him by noon. By twelve-thirty he had shaved, bathed, dressed and was taking coffee at the eatery next door prior to making the day's first patrol of the streets when the door opened and the young woman entered.

Seated with his back against the wall, as always, Ashton glanced up and felt his heart skip one full beat.

It was Barbara Kincaid.

CHAPTER 4

RIDERS FROM TWENTY MILE

'You've grown quiet, Cord.'

'I guess maybe I have. . . .'

This was loco, Ashton thought. Only five minutes back in the company of the girl he had never quit thinking about, and he was acting as tongue-tied as some green kid out on his first date.

Why so? Was it because he'd not expected to meet her quite this soon? Or maybe he'd been thrown off balance by her candid admission she'd come to town specifically to see him?

But the simpler and more probable cause for his odd reaction became clear when, seated here opposite him now, he saw she appeared somehow even more beautiful than he remembered.

He studied her closely as she smiled at him and sipped her coffee. Tall, statuesque and elegant even in a simple checked shirt and tailored riding trousers, Barbara Kincaid looked exactly what she was, a lady and a thoroughbred.

With shoulder-length hair and brilliant blue eyes that were a family characteristic, she was like the stuff that dreams were made of.

Yet this was no dream.

She was a flesh and blood woman who'd made this journey into town just to seek him out . . . yet all he could do was stare and feel his insides knot like a clenched fist.

Yet she saved the day when, as though aware of his feelings, she began conversing in the most natural way, her tones clipped by the expensive accent she'd acquired during four years at a finishing college in the East, her face animated in a way he remembered only too well.

Barbara Kincaid spoke of day-to-day matters, of life on the Silver Dollar, her brother, the cattle business and many other both ordinary and commonplace things – with every topic seeming to hold tremendous signficicance for her audience of one, simply because she was doing the talking.

Then, gradually, as time went by, Cord felt himself at last begin to feel at ease. He lighted a cigar and even managed a relaxed smile at some quip she made.

'Oh, that's much better, Cord. That smile is more like the way I remember you.'

It went easier after that and, at her insistence, he began relating a little of what had occupied him since quitting Sugar Creek. He focused on personal matters and humorous aspects of his career while studiously avoiding any reference to the blood and violence that could be part of his profession. He could always rely upon the sensation-hungry Western press to guarantee that Cord Ashton's exploits were always too well and too widely publicised.

They were on their second coffees before she posed the question he knew had to come.

'Cord, what brought you back? I mean . . . really?'

He looked her straight in the eye and lied. 'This place needed me, Barbara.'

'Is that the only reason?'

'There's always more than one other reason for doing anything, I guess,' he replied evasively.

Her 'Oh' was a small sound in the sudden silence. She stirred her coffee thoughtfully for a time before glancing up again to meet his gaze. 'Well, whatever the reason, I'm very pleased you are back.'

What exactly did she mean by that? Ashton told himself it could mean very little, or possibly everything. He wasn't sure he really wanted to know.

He said, 'Your brother isn't pleased.'

Her face fell, the brightness leaving her cheeks. 'No . . . no, he told me you'd already met. Was it very bad, Cord? I know how Stirling can be. . . .'

Ashton shrugged. 'We never did get along. I put that down to the fact that Stirling can't accept restrictions to his life and I represent a restriction.'

'He's always been that way. I suppose that comes from having too much, too soon.'

'Maybe.' Cord frowned thoughtfully. 'Yet the other night when we met it seemed he was even more set against me than ever. I really can't figure that one.'

'But you do have some idea . . . I could always tell with you. . . .'

He was considering his response when a shadow filled the sunlit doorway. A man stood there, handsome and slim-hipped with good shoulders and a tied-down gun. His face was tanned and his manner exuded natural authority. His garb was dark and expensive.

'Why . . . Brett!' Barbara said quickly, rising. 'How nice to see you.'

Ashton rose as Brett Cody crossed to the table. He'd always got along reasonably well with the youthful boss of the Bar 50 Ranch in the past, yet Cody's look today seemed unfriendly and he made no attempt to offer his hand as he grunted, 'Sheriff.'

'Howdy, Brett.'

Cody turned to the girl. 'I rode across to visit you this morning, Barbara. Stirling told me you'd come into town.'

'And you came all the way in just to see me?' The girl smiled. 'Why, that's very flattering, Brett. Don't you think so, Cord?'

'I guess I'd better be on my way,' Cord said, collecting his hat.

'Oh no, Cord,' the girl protested. 'Brett will have coffee with us, won't you, Brett?'

Cody was plainly reluctant but the girl insisted and Ashton found himself back in his chair studying the man in silence as the waitress fetched fresh coffee.

Cody was a type rarely encountered in this wild corner of the West. Son of a wealthy and aristocratic father he'd been sent East for his education where he'd been instructed in the art of being a gentleman. He was an accomplished horseman, top-class swordsman and a crack pistol shot.

Ashton was already aware that, allegedly because of high living and poor management, the Bar 50 had been running downhill since he was here last. He'd also learned that Cody had killed two miners in a gun duel here in Sugar Creek some months back. Studying the man closely now it seemed he sensed a flinty maturity about him that had not been evident before.

Yet there was also a hint of weakness in Cody's makeup somewhere that seemed more noticeable today than it had been.

Whatever the case, Brett Cody was now undoubtedly a formidable presence bordering upon the hostile, and Ashton was made well aware of that in the following minutes of stilted conversation during which the man restricted himself mostly to monosyllables and an attitude of scowling superiority.

And suddenly Cord was reminded of what Stirling Kincaid had remarked about Brett being a gentleman . . . a man of background and distinction, somebody of Barbara's own class. And sensed the man might well have also added, 'Unlike you, Ashton . . . gunman, peace officer . . . notorious identity. . . ?

Once more he rose to go.

'Don't go, do stay a little longer,' the woman urged. 'Please, Cord?'

'Sorry, but I have work to do.' He spoke more tersely than he intended. 'It's been nice catching up, Barbara.' A pause. 'Brett.'

'Take care, Cord,' the girl called after him, but Brett Cody stared sullenly and said nothing.

Fitting hat to head as he went out, Ashton peered back through the windows and carried away a picture of the couple seated there together; the rich, young, educated woman from the Silver Dollar Ranch with the handsome and educated young man from the sprawling Bar 50.

Made for each other . . . surely?

He suddenly suspected now it had been a mistake to come back to this town – no matter what his reason. He felt this as he trod the plankwalks in the sun, glancing neither left nor right. He'd believed he was coming back to complete unfinished business, now understood that the need to see her again was likely much closer to the truth. What had he expected? That she might toss aside a rich and powerful man who wanted to marry her for a gunman wearing a star?

Reality, Ashton! What happened your sense of reality?

And yet even as he walked on, castigating himself for ever having come back to Sugar Creek – for whatever reason – he realized with a sudden jolt that it wasn't that simple.

He couldn't quit.

So what if he'd come here for the wrong reason? Two wrongs didn't make a right and the one thing certain was that if he were to quit Sugar Creek right now he would be guilty of the biggest mistake any lawman worthy of the name could make.

So he was hurting right now. He'd quit at the wrong time before and would not make that mistake again. This troubled town needed Cord Ashton and he owed it to Sugar Creek to see it through.

They arrived in town in force mostly by chance one week later, the wild hellions from the Twenty Mile, the prospectors who came down out of the Rattlesnake Hills, the thirsty cowboys from the Silver Dollar, Bar Twenty and the Double S. They came in their numbers to drink, carouse, wench or howl at the moon while quite a number admitted showing up for quite another reason – to take a close-up look at the new tough sheriff.

Ashton didn't disappoint them.

From just after sunrise, in black broadcloth jacket and pearl-grey Stetson, he put himself on public view, patrolling Federation Street, visiting the saloons, cat-houses and gambling halls, jugging anyone who looked like he might need it, cracking heads on public thoroughfares and ready and able to nip all and any trouble in the bud before it was able to get properly started.

He walked slowly but packed a fast gun.

As though in reaction to the clamp-down, trouble flickered and flared frequently along lower Federation Sreet and below the Deadline, but never really caught fire. There was rebellious talk city-wide and rumours of fast guns and sheriff-killers converging on the sprawling town on the plains, yet somehow they failed to materialize . . . while the sheriff was very rarely off their streets.

Through it all, Ashton was a grimly confident and assured figure, yet did not believe for one moment that his crack-down was going to prove the magical one-dose-cures-all-ills purgative for this sprawling boom town.

For there had been powerful forces at work in Sugar Creek before his return and until these re-emerged to challenge him he was not about to claim even token victories in the battle to create a good, strong and law-abiding community.

As he prowled the streets at midday and midnight with his Colt riding his thigh, Ashton kept his mind on his job and paid heed to his inner thoughts, his senses and his hunches.

He congratulated himself for the vast improvement in life, commerce and profit in Sugar Creek, yet never walked blindly into a dark alley or took one reckless chance any place.

Every hour of experience he'd had on streets like these told him clearly that, while small-timers and petty thieves might be griping and even howling against his campaign, other elements were quietly and competently planning the counter-attack.

There was a sense in him that warned that the big men were all waiting for the next man to do something about him, but as time went by and the jailhouse bulged with offenders, whispers and rumours began to coalesce until the stormy night the sheriff sat at his desk sifting fact from fiction and at last came up with a name.

'Kell McCrow' was the whisper which in time hardened into a suspicion . . . the same Kell McCrow who had gunned Sheriff Barney Tobin down on these very streets – supposedly a kill on contract job arranged by the back-room bosses of Sugar Creek when his law enforcement interfered with those who regarded themselves as the true masters of Sugar Creek. . . .

McCrow didn't show that Saturday night and it might have been because of this that serious trouble failed to break out despite the numbers in town. It was like the dark side of town was waiting to see whether or not the McCrow rumour was real or just that, another lousy rumour.

Most of those players were still to be seen loafing

around Sugar Creek's streets the following afternoon, many nursing savage hangovers and lamenting empty purses, when word flashed down Federation that McCrow had arrived with Curly Flynn and a few other boys and were taking a drink below the Line at the Deadline Saloon.

Ashton was at the jailhouse bringing the charge book up to date when the news of McCrow's arrival reached him through an apprehensive Mayor Don Garroway. The mayor appeared puzzled when Ashton merely murmured, 'Thank you, Mayor,' and continued writing.

'They looked like they are looking for trouble and loaded for bear, Sheriff,' the mayor insisted.

'Most likely, Mayor Garroway. Now, if you'll excuse me I have work to complete here.'

The mayor left, scratching his neck and looking deflated, leaving the lawman to continue until the chore was completed. Only then did Ashton close over the buckram bound ledger and, placing it in the desk drawer, rose and moved to stand in the doorway.

There were any number of people on Federation Street but the mood was quiet. In far distance, the Rattlesnake Hills were a deep blue against the pale wash of the sky. Long afternoon shadows crept down Sugar Creek's main stem, the stucco walls of the Prairie Flower Saloon glowing pink in the sun's late rays.

All appeared peaceful down below the Deadline.

After several minutes Ashton came back into the

office to stand staring at the adobe wall by the gunrack. Scratched into the plaster were the names of the lawmen who tried to bring law and order to the town. They had failed, mainly because they were not gunfighters – unlike Cord Ashton.

The last name recorded, scratched with a nail, was that of Barney Tobin.

Ashton stroked his jaw. He had known Barney Tobin, a quiet and deliberate man who had once operated a small store down on Kiowa Street. After much persuasion the then council had persuaded Tobin to pin on a badge at fifty dollars per week and found. They'd laid Tobin to rest three weeks later when Kell McCrow killed him. He left a wife and three children.

Cord quit the office soon after to make his regular twilight patrol.

He seemed not to notice the expectant knots of men who watched his every step as he in turn looked in on the Prairie Flower, the Hard Luck and the Green before heading for the Deadline.

It was as he was approaching his objective that he happened to glance upwards to sight the tall figure of a man leaning over the balcony of the Federation Hotel.

Stirling Kincaid stood hatless in the late afternoon light with a slim cigar clamped in his teeth and the man was smiling. It was an odd, wolfish kind of smile and it was directed at the lawman. It wasn't until the town-tamer felt the full impact of that intensely predatory look that understanding hit like a bullet.

This man had come to town to see McCrow kill him!

For just a moment Ashton was shaken. He had never been in any doubt about how Barbara's brother felt towards him, their long-time antipathy was mutual. But until now he'd never suspected the man hated him enough to want him dead.

A jarring moment, yet it passed swiftly because the town-tamer willed it away.

He'd walked the streets of the West too long to feel vulnerable before anything or anyone. He was intent right now only on completing the patrol he'd set out upon here, exactly as if that figure on the balcony did not exist. He's come down here to check out the roughneck saloons of Sugar Creek and that was what he would do. Every one.

He imagined he heard a mocking chuckle drift down as he walked by the Federation, the stiffening evening breeze tugging at his four-in-hand tie.

He did not even glance up.

Eventually crossing the Deadline he continued on at a steady, unhurried pace in the direction of the Sierra Saloon where a long line of Twenty Mile horses could be seen drawn up at the hitchrack.

He walked right on by.

It wasn't until he was passing the burnt-out skeleton of the old limestone bakery that he sighted the figure standing in what remained of the doorway, arms folded across his chest, a thin cheroot dangling from a razor-slash mouth.

His hand instinctively dropped to gun handle as he halted, his voice carrying clearly.

'Out of your regular territory some, aren't you, Jack?'

Wild Jack Mason's eyes were almost colourless in the fading light. 'Just taking the air, Ashton. No new law agin' that, is there?'

Ashton glanced back at the Sierra. Nothing happening there – no sign of back-up guns should this man make a play. He couldn't quite read this gunman in that moment. It could be Mason intended to challenge simply out of vanity and ego. Then again, this anything but accidental meeting could be a test, an opportunity for the shootist to size him up against some future time when they might square off. With this breed you could never be certain.

He said quietly, 'You've got the right to be any place you want – most times, that is. But when things are tight I don't care to have someone like you at my back. Now, I'm heading for the Sierra Saloon which means that if you stayed here you would be at my back.' A deliberate pause. 'That does not suit.'

'You askin' me to move on, Sheriff?'

'No. Ordering.'

Wild Jack Mason straightened, hands unfolding to hang by his sides. His eyes now blazed at Ashton with full candlepower, but the lawman was a rock, indifferent. A full twenty seconds passed before Mason suddenly shrugged, fixed his grin back in place and emerged fully from his doorway.

'Hell, Sheriff, if you want me to move that bad, I'll move.'

Hooking thumbs in shell-belt the hardcase sauntered off north along Federation, whistling tunelessly between his teeth. Features blank, Ashton watched him go, then turned and put the man from his thoughts and continued on to the saloon.

The Sierra Saloon was a converted barn and still smelt and looked like one despite the long bar, the rough tables and the even rougher-looking crowd. The place had an earther floor, cheap whiskey and a bad reputation county-wide.

And on this particular evening it boasted a killer amongst its clients.

Threading his way slowly between the tables towards the bar, Ashton's quick eye picked out Kell McCrow seated amongst a bunch of Twenty Mile riders at a long table by the west wall.

McCrow was staring fixedly at Ashton as the saloon began to quieten. He was a dark and ugly young man with the black dash of a moustache. He wore a single gold earring that caught the fading light in silent bursts of flame.

He dressed all in black and sported a white-handled Colt.

Ashton moved on unhurriedly to the bar and nodded his head when the barkeep silently held up a shot glass. He had no intention of forcing a showdown with the gunner, he even made the effort to thrust Sheriff Barney Tobin's death from his mind – for now. That was in the past and he didn't yet know the full facts of it. The situation here and now was that he was the peace officer of Sugar Creek and officially had no beef with this killer, providing he didn't break any laws.

There was a warning whirr from a battered old clock above the bar mirror as the strikers lifted from the chimes. The mechanical sound ended with a sudden sharp click and the six gongs rang out, seemingly leaving the Sierra even quieter than before.

A man coughed drily and the man at the piano began to play, immediately thought better of it and went back to chewing his nails and squinting at the tall figure of the lawman.

Ashton was all too well remembered here from before, and nobody understood why he'd come back.

The sheriff alone knew that.

Seated at Mason's elbow Curly Flynn's mood was sour and growing meaner. His face blotched from too much liquor, it had been Flynn doing most of the big talk about what McCrow would do to Ashton when they finally met face-to-face, and the bunch had made the long ride in from the Twenty Mile in the hope of being on hand when the guns started going off.

But McCrow's sullen silence and the way he didn't

seem inclined to meet Ashton's occasional chill stare from the bar raised all sorts of doubts in the hard-case's mind.

Until eventually he had to speak up. 'Hey, Kell, ain't you got nothin' to say to this tinstar?'

'Why don't you shut your mouth, Curly?' McCrow licked a brown paper quirley into a neat cylinder and felt his pockets for vestas. His gaze returned to the figure at the bar. 'I'll talk to him when I'm good and ready, is when.'

That didn't satisfy Curly Flynn.

'Damnitall, Kell, just look at the way he's standin' over there, will you? Lordin' it over everybody, so he is. If we don't talk up he'll think he's got us buffaloed.'

'He's wrong if he thinks that.'

'Then show the tinstar son of a bitch, man,' Flynn said loudly. It was too loud. Ashton heard him.

'What was that, cowboy?' he said quietly. 'You referring to me?'

'What if I was?' Flynn retorted, boosted by whiskey courage and emboldened by McCrow's presence.

Ashton had been ready to quit the saloon moments before. But now he set his glass aside and began threading his way through the tables towards them. Flynn turned to nudge McCrow, but the gunman shoved him away angrily. Flynn turned appealingly to the Twenty Mile riders but all were focused upon Ashton by this.

'I thought I gave you a lesson recent, cowboy,'

Ashton said, coming to a halt before their table. 'Seems you're a hard man to get through to. Or stupid!'

Curly Flynn's face flushed hotly. This wasn't turning out the way he figured. Over recent days he'd been working on Kell McCrow in an attempt to get him to go after Ashton. He had not anticipated a repetition of his own embarrassing set-to with the badgeman.

He was out on a limb with no way of getting off it – other than by bluff.

'Back off, lawdog!' he snarled. 'Git, before you buy more trouble than you can handle!'

Ashton glanced across at McCrow. The gunner stared back with a look that revealed nothing.

Ashton nodded. 'I don't intend busting your fool head again, Flynn. And I don't intend cluttering up jailhouse space with you either. That only leaves posting. You're posted from town as of right now.'

'Posted?' echoed Flynn. 'What the sweet Judas does that mean?'

'It means the man is barrin' you, Curly,' Kell McCrow supplied, staring at Ashton.

'Barrin' me?' Flynn was outraged. 'You can't bar a man from a town. Nobody's got that kind of power.'

Ashton tapped the badge on his vest. 'This says I've got the power.' He snapped his fingers. 'All right, I'll have your gun and you will mount and ride.'

It seemed a painful physical efffort for Flynn to

drag his gaze off Ashton to the face of the man at his side. 'Kell—'

'Hush your mouth!' McCrow hissed. He turned back to Ashton, face grim now. 'But he's right, Ashton. You don't have the right.'

Something clicked in Cord Ashton's head. He believed he'd put the sheriff's death from his mind but McCrow's defiance reminded him he was dealing with a lawman-killer, surely the breed at the top of his hate list.

'Are you interfering with the discharge of my duties, McCrow?' His voice sounded flat, his face without expression.

Curly Flynn's mocking laugh was soft, yet sounded loud in the stillness. 'Yeah, that's what the man is doin' sure enough—'

'Shut up!' McCrow snarled. 'I'll do my own talkin' cowboy. I'm tellin' you straight you ain't got the authority to bar Curly from town, lawman!'

'Wrong!' Ashton rapped. 'I have the authority and I'm using it. Now you're both posted from town!'

McCrow went white and Curly Flynn blinked while the Twenty Mile crew stiffened as one. Cord had been ready to take on two gunslingers if needs be, but not a mob. . . .

His right hand blurred faster than the eye could follow and came up holding a cocked .45.

In the stunned silence that followed his voice cracked like a whip.

'Flynn, McCrow, you are posted from town for the

period of one month. You will quit town now and the rest of your bunch will quit town with you. And when I say now, that's what I mean. Move!'

'Judas Priest, don't let the bastard do that, Kell!' Curly Flynn raged just one split second before Ashton's Colt blurred and smashed against the side of his skull, felling him like a dead man.

Everybody was backing up as the sheriff deliberately pulled his gun hammer on to full cock. He waved the weapon slowly. 'Think in terms of seconds . . . if the whole pack of you aren't out on the street inside five seconds this thing is going to start going off!'

They believed him. Surely only a fool would not. And when a white-lipped Curly Flynn abruptly staggered to his feet and headed hastily for the swinging doors it was like a dam-break, the rat-tat of so many boot-heels almost drowning out the derisive taunts and shouts of the barflies who were enjoying the best entertainment seen here in months.

Calmly and deliberately, Ashton pumped a shot into the ceiling then trailed the last white-faced waddy outside. The street was alive with men on horseback and others struggling to get mounted. Another shot . . . and everybody finally managed to fill leather to go storming away with chippies from the bordello opposite cheering and jeering from their balcony even though unaware of what exactly was taking place.

Until at last Ashton stood alone in the middle of

the street . . . Just himself and a Colt .45.

Squinting through dust his gaze flicked automatically back to the balcony of the Federation Hotel three doors along where he could see Stirling Kincaid still standing up there gripping the railing, his face a mask of rage and hate.

'Hard luck, Kincaid,' he muttered to himself. His face once more expressionless as he made his way back from the Sierra Saloon, the sheriff of Sugar Creek, walking neither fast nor slow, made his way back along Federation Street for the central block.

CHAPTER 5

WAY OF A LAWMAN

'The question as I see it,' storekeeper Marsh Toomey declared at the meeting of the Sugar Creek Council the following morning, 'is whether the sheriff has the power to do it or not.'

'He's already done it,' declared Mayor Don Garroway, seated at the head of the long table in the council chambers. 'He's posted McCrow from town and that's how it stands.'

Banker Jobe Calvin smiled cynically.

'Marsh, you should know as well as any of us that the only legal power worth a cuss in Sugar Creek is whatever can be enforced.'

He paused to glance meaningfully around at his fellow councillors before continuing.

'Up until the time the sheriff responded to our

plea to come back we didn't even have enough law around here to prevent a sheriff getting killed. But now we have law and I for one don't see one lick of sense in quibbling with it.'

Heads nodded in agreement and Ike Heller of the Sugar Creek Stage Company, declared, 'That is so, Marsh. When we swore in Sheriff Ashton, we did so with full confidence based upon his previous record here and his expressed interest in our town. I feel the sheriff is doing an abolutely sterling job.'

'I ain't arguing with that, Ike,' said Toomey. 'All I'm saying is that you never can tell where this sort of thing might lead. The sheriff has posted McCrow and Curly Flynn out of town, which might be a good thing. But who's to say who could be next?' The diminutive storekeeper spread his hands. 'Heck, he might get around to postin' anybody – even one of us.'

Councillors made derisive sounds and Garroway gavelled for order.

'Marsh,' he said with a puzzled frown, 'this doesn't sound like you at all. You were as keen as any of us to sign Cord Ashton on yet now you seem to be having second thoughts. Why, man, tell us that? We all believe the sheriff won't exceed his authority so why are you taking this stand?'

'I've a right to my opinion,' Toomey insisted.

'Sure you have,' Garroway agreed. 'But I'm not certain that what you're spouting is your opinion.'

Everybody stared at the speaker. 'What do you

mean by that?' asked liveryman Vic Kramer.

'Yeah,' chimed in the fiesty Toomey. 'Why don't you tell us what you mean by that crack?'

Garroway focused upon Toomey. 'I just happened to walk by your house last night, Marsh . . . and I saw Stirling Kincaid's flash horse tied up to your front fence.'

Toomey seemed to pale. 'Well, what if it was?'

'That's what we want you to tell us,' Garroway answered.

Toomey stared from face to face before he finally sighed and shrugged and leaned back in his chair. 'Yeah, all right, might as well admit it. Kincaid called to see me last night.' A pause. 'About Ashton.'

'Figured as much,' said Garroway. 'And can I make a guess, Marsh? Kincaid persuaded you to call this here meeting in the hope of cancelling Ashton's contract?'

Toomey nodded, yet his voice was uncertain as he spoke.

'Stirling has got some mighty hard ways about him at times. . . .' He paused and looked from face to face. 'I guess I don't have to tell any of you that?'

Heads shook around the table. All here knew Stirling only too well. There was a time when the man had sat on the council but in those days it had been a one-man council. Kincaid's. Overbearing and autocratic he'd run both council and town with ruthless authority until they resisted him in strength on a single issue, at which time he resigned and washed his hands of the council, permanently.

The rift all boiled down to the fact that the councillors were determined to represent their voters while Kincaid intended it to be simply and solely an instrument of his will.

The councillors hadn't consulted Kincaid when they made their approach to Ashton, knowing what his reaction must be. They had found the courage to take this step but there wasn't one of them not afraid of their former associate and there was a whiff of fear in the room now as they waited for Marsh Toomey to continue.

The man talked straight.

'I'll level with you. Stirling has told me he'd withdraw all the Silver Dollar business from my store unless I move to have the sheriff suspended.'

Calvin sighed gustily.

'Guess none of us is too much surprised to hear that, huh?'

Heads shook and Toomey looked puzzled. 'Damnit, I don't figure why Stirling has come down so hard on the sheriff. What's he got again him anyways?'

'Mebbe I can answer that,' weighed in Clancy Ross of the American House Hotel. 'A clerk of mine happened to overhear part of a confab between Stirling and the sheriff the night Ashton arrived. It seemed there was some discussion about Kincaid's sister. Jenkins didn't catch it all but he sure heard Kincaid warn the sheriff to keep away from Barbara.'

'Sheriff Ashton and Barbara Kincaid?' Garroway said, surprised. 'I never heard anything about that.'

'They were friends as I recall,' supplied Vic Kramer. 'I never heard anything more than that.'

'Sounds like there could well be something more the way Kincaid has been acting,' opined Clancy Ross.

They were silent for a time, each man considering what had been revealed and what it might mean in terms of the immediate future. When they began talking again they did so frankly, daring for the first time to openly criticize Stirling Kincaid in light of his recent behaviour along with his hostile attitude to Ashton now.

In the end the mayor summed up. 'Seems to me Stirling has decided he wants to be free to make his own rules and laws and go his own way. That can't be allowed to happen. Of course had he been able to offer us more protection against the cowboys and miners, then maybe we'd look on things different. But he's said openly that if the wild men don't interfere with business in town then he's happy to let them do pretty much as they please.'

'That's not good enough!' Garroway stated emphatically. 'I'm not saying that hiring a town-tamer with unlimited powers is the best of all systems. But I see it as better than walking in fear of our lives . . . or seeing a fine sheriff shot down in the street like a dog!'

'Couldn't agree more,' Ike Heller supported. 'I'm

moving a motion that we register a vote of full confidence in the sheriff and pass it on to him.'

'Well said, Ike,' said Garroway. 'All right, let's have a show of hands.'

Every hand but Marsh Toomey's went up. The little man was concerned about his loss of business should the Silver Dollar blacklist his place. Yet in the last moments the little man was seen to raise his hand and the vote was declared unanimous.

'I'm right proud of you, councillors . . . every man Jack of you!' Garroway declared. And to show he meant what he said he took them all down for a drink at the Prairie Flower Saloon where already the gamblers were laying odds that Kell McCrow would show up long before his month's posting was up. With his gun, of course.

Cord Ashton sat in the sun on the porch of the Sugar Creek jailhouse in broadcloth suit, polished black boots and his familiar low-crowned grey hat. He smoked a long cigar and watched the activities of Sugar Creek in the afternoon: the bustle down Federation Street of horsemen and wagons and citizens afoot, the loafers along the galleries, that bunch of miners from the Rattlesnake Hills pitching horseshoes in the vacant lot alongside the Prairie Flower Saloon.

He grinned as he saw the game interrupted when two of Kitty Dechine's girls strolled by in their fancy clothes and picture hats. A burly, bearded miner made a pretend lunge at the girls, then staggered when a furled parasol cracked him sharply across the head, drawing mocking laughter from companions loafing in the nearby shade.

Ashton turned his head as Tab Merrill emerged from the jailhouse. Old Tab, who had been hired as turnkey by the council, held a broom in one hand and was swabbing sweat from his forehead.

'She's all shipshape inside now, Sheriff,' he announced, 'so I'll be gettin' along.'

'Thank you, Mr Merrill.'

'Pleasure, Sheriff. Oh, and by the way, Lon Green just rode in out back. Says he's got something for you.'

Ashton nodded and rose as the old man trudged off. With a last glance at the street he turned into the doorway, crossed the freshly swept office and passed down the corridor between the cells.

'Hey, Sheriff!' yelled a hoarse voice. 'When you gonna let me out?'

Cord paused before the grilled door of the cell that held the jailhouse's only prisoner at the moment, Tinpot Tolliver, town drunk and casual piano player at the Sierra Saloon. Tinpot's offence last night occurred when, far into his cups, he had fallen through a store window.

'Why, I guess that depends, Mr Tolliver.'

'On what, Sheriff?'

'Why, on whether you intend mending your ways, of course.'

Tolliver clapped a hand to his heart. 'I swear I ain't gonna touch another drop so long as I live, Sheriff.'

'Well, in that case,' Ashton murmured and to the prisoner's astonishment he unlocked the door and swung it wide.

Tolliver blinked owlishly. 'You mean you're really setting me loose, Sheriff?'

'On your personal assurance that you will be of good behaviour,' Ashton said, poker-faced, knowing full well that Tolliver's skinny legs would take him directly from the jail to the nearest saloon by the shortest possible route.

'Yahoo!' the whiskey-soak exulted, snatching up his battered top hat and jumping out the door before the law could change its mind. He paused, poised for flight. 'Just goes to show how wrong you can be about a feller, don't it?'

'How's that?'

'Well, everybody is saying how hard and mean you are, Sheriff, but they won't be hearing any of that buffalo dust from yours truly from now on in.'

'Thank you, Mr Tolliver.'

'Hey, Cord!' Lon Green's voice sounded from in back. 'I got somethin' to show you.'

Ashton turned to respond but a suddenly sober drunkard touched his arm.

'Jest afore you go, Sheriff, you done me a good turn so I'll do the same for you. Last night there was some Twenty Mile riders in the Sierra and they was sayin' as how Kell McCrow is fixin' to come to town gunnin' after you. Real soon, they claimed, so mebbe you'd better—'

'Thanks, Mr Tolliver,' Cord interrupted, and went on through to the back. Lon Green's saddle-horse was tied up at the railing of the jailhouse corral. The boy stood within the corral, holding a lead rope attached to a piebald horse.

'What have you got there, Lon?'

'Come take a look.'

Ashton crossed the yard and climbed to the top rail. 'Well, I'm looking but I don't see much of anything,' he said.

'Well, if that don't beat all,' Lon said, looking hurt. 'I go to all that trouble fetchin' you a good remount and that's all the thanks I get.'

'That's mine?' Ashton said, dropping into the yard and approaching the animal.

'You bet it is. Best horse I've handled in months and he's all yours.'

He sobered. 'I can't accept a gift like that, Lon.' He ran his eyes over the animal and realized it was of far higher quality than he'd first thought. 'I need a good remount, sure, but I'll buy it from you.'

The boy argued. He persuaded Cord to ride the colt around the yard several times by which time he knew he must have it. Ashton made a decent bid only to be told by Lon he would allow him to buy him a drink and the deal would be sealed.

Touched and impressed, Ashton sighed, agreed and they headed off for the saloon.

It was cool and pleasant in the Prairie Flower as they breasted the bar, Lon Green with a mug of beer, Ashton a shot glass of whiskey sour. It was a couple of days since Ashton had seen the boy and quickly realized Lon had something more than horses on his mind by the time they were halfway through their drinks.

'Something bothering you, Lon?'

Lon met his gaze levelly. 'You had some trouble the other afternoon, Cord?'

'You mean McCrow?'

'Uh-huh.'

'Nothing much to speak of.'

'He's a bad one, Cord. Real bad.'

'So they tell me.'

'Hey, don't be offhand with me, Cord. I reckon you must be thinking plenty about that gunner.'

A glint of humour showed in Ashton's eyes. 'What is this, boy? You taking to playing nursemaid?'

The youth didn't answer his smile. 'They are laying odds he'll come in to get you and I want to be there to back your play when he does. Remember I'm good with a gun . . . since you taught me.'

Ashton stared at the youth and once again was thinking just how few friends he'd cultivated in his lonely lawman's life. Lon had slipped under his guard, but that didn't mean he would accept his offer.

'No,' he said firmly. 'I appreciate the thought but I don't need help. I know I taught you how to handle a gun to protect yourself, but not to risk your life against bad men.'

'You do it all the time, Cord.'

'I do it because somebody has to, not for any other reason.' He paused, and when he continued, his manner was thoughtful. 'It can be a mighty lonely life, Lon, and surely not for boys like you.'

'But McCrow—'

'I said no!' Ashton said in a tone that closed the subject. 'But you can do one thing for me, Lon. Tell me whatever you know about McCrow and Sheriff Tobin.'

Green sighed in resignation. 'OK, Cord, what do you want to know?'

'How did he kill the sheriff? Was it a fair fight?'

'Well, I guess it was fair insofar as McCrow called the sheriff out. But hell, Cord, what sort of fair fight is it between a gunshark and a feller like Barney Tobin who only ever used his gun to bang drunks on the head with?'

Ashton nodded slowly. He knew he was hearing the story right, maybe for the first time. A top gunslinger going up against a simple citizen was sure something that would be in his mind if and when McCrow should be dumb enough to return to town before his full month was up.

CHAPTER 6

AT THE SILVER DOLLAR

It was Wednesday afternoon and Brett Cody was just quitting the Bar 50 and his way to the Silver Dollar Ranch where he had an invitation to supper, when he sighted Jobe Calvin's surrey swinging down the trail from the direction of town.

Cody frowned as he closed the ranch gate behind him and muttered something under his breath. Damn Calvin! It seemed every time he turned around these days the banker was there at his elbow complaining about his mortgage payments and his overdraft at the bank. It was getting so that he was avoiding coming into Sugar Creek in case he should meet the banker on the street. He tried to muster up a grin as the banker's rig drew up alongside, yet it didn't quite come off.

'Mr Calvin,' he said warily.

'Just caught you, eh, Mr Cody?' Calvin appeared serious under his black hat. It seemed months since Cody had seen the man smile.

'Guess you did,' Cody relied flatly. 'I'm just on my way to the Kincaids'.' Then he added deliberately, 'I'm running late.'

'Well, I wouldn't want to delay you, young man, but I'm sure you know why I've come to see you?'

'I reckon I can guess.'

'I'm quite sure you can. Look here, Mr Cody, I don't like to badger a man but you must realize something must be done about your state of affairs, and quickly. The last time we spoke you promised you would be depositing within two weeks. That was three weeks back and I still haven't—'

'I know, damnit. But I explained before that I'm having a bad season.'

Brushing flies from his face, the banker looked over the broad acres of the Bar 50, before replying. 'I can't understand why that should be so, Mr Cody. Other ranchers don't appear to be having your problems this year.'

'Are you hinting I'm a bad manager?'

'I'm suggesting you could do far better by attempting to live within your means and perhaps applying yourself more dilligently to the operation of your ranch.'

Brett Cody bit back the hasty retort. Trouble was, he reflected, Calvin was right. Cody knew he lived far beyond his means and had no real aptitude for the ranch life. He felt it was his destiny to sit back and enjoy the good life of a wealthy aristocrat while others did the sweating. He'd been able to do just that for three years after his father passed away, but over recent months his high living and neglect of ranch affairs had caught up with him and there was the feeling that events were closing in on him.

But there was a way out, he reminded himself, forcing a confident smile.

'Give me another month, Mr Calvin. That's all I ask.'

'Can you guarantee your situation will improve in that time?'

'Sure.'

'Can you explain how?'

'Damn you, Calvin, the way you hound a man—'

'Let's have no harsh words. If you have a means of adjusting your affairs then I have the right to know what they might be.'

'All right, damnit! The fact is, inside a month I expect to be engaged to Miss Kincaid.'

The banker's pinched face lost its tight-lipped look. 'Oh, well, if that is the case then it would certainly make a great difference, I'm sure.' Then his eyes became sharp again behind steel-rimmed spectacles. 'You honestly believe this event will take place?'

'I said so, didn't I?'

'Very well, we'll let it go at that,' said the banker, lifting the reins. 'But of course if there is any change of plans I would expect to be informed.'

'There won't be any changes,' Brett snapped back and with a light pressure of the knees sent the big stallion jumping away.

'Bloodsucker!' he mouthed as he saw the banker's rig swinging on to the town trail. Then turning ahead again, he gazed over the low range of hills and felt the bite of uncertainty. For two months he'd been attempting to slip a ring on the girl's finger but without success. Recently he'd asked her straight out if anything was wrong, but as usual she had been evasive. He couldn't figure it out. She knew he wanted to get married, they were surely well suited, so he believed. And importantly, Stirling was totally in support of their marrying.

Then why the delay?

He brooded about that while he rode until his head ached from it, yet still couldn't put his finger on what was amiss. He'd not mentioned his concern to Stirling, yet passing through the Silver Dollar's main gate a short time later he sensed that tonight might be the right time to do so. If something was wrong then Stirling would know exactly how to rectify it. He always did.

Cord Ashton occupied a chair in the shade of the *Great West* newspaper office on the main street of town. The sheriff was in shirtsleeves buttoned at the wrist and sat with his left leg comfortably bent and the right straight out before him.

He mostly sat in that position whenever he relaxed for it assured quick and easy access to the Colt .45 in his right holster – should it be needed.

The sheriff was not expecting trouble but experience had taught him this was often a time when a man had to be at his most careful.

He smiled at the thought and told himself, 'You weren't this careful when you were younger, Cord.' But then, everything changed as a man grew older and some towns grew wilder and meaner.

Towns like this one.

Lighting up, he inhaled deeply and glanced along the dusty street. This had been a wild place when he'd taken over before and he'd had more than a few close calls while bringing it to heel. He frowned and sat up straighter to reach for his cigars. He couldn't give any clear reason why Sugar Creek felt any more dangerous today than it had this time last week – or even back when he'd done did his first stint here. So why was he edgy today, seemingly without reason?

He nodded slowly, telling himself that maybe he did know why. He'd come back here telling himself he was doing the right thing by a potentially decent town and its many good people. But that wasn't strictly the truth. The real reason was far simpler.

Barbara.

He'd missed her too much and had quit his last

posting with some foolish notion that by coming here things might somehow change for them and—

'Howdy, Sheriff. You got time to take a look at my manifest for the stockyards I got here?'

It was a hard luck rancher from Cattle Creek who interrupted his thoughts. The man appeared surprised when the usually sober lawman gave him a grin and rose quickly.

Cord acted pleased to see the man, and was.

For this was what he did best and what he was here for, he reminded himself as they headed indoors. The day to day demands of the job. Everything outside his work was . . . what, Cord? Pie in the sky? Dreaming? He didn't want to believe that but maybe it would be better in the long run if he could.

For even if he still loved her that didn't mean she had to be in love with him.

The Kincaid ranch house was the finest in Ramrod Valley and its splendid dining-room was something very special to those select few who ever got to see it.

Thirty feet long by twenty wide it discreetly yet effectively reflected the wealth the family had been acquiring ever since old man Kincaid had first come to the valley twenty years before.

The centrepiece was a massive oak table flanked by hand-carved, high-backed chairs. There were twin scarlet sofas with scrolled ends, chairs in red and gold brocade which spoke of wealth and fine taste.

There were numerous dressers and small tables, a

marble topped bureau, china lamps of various sizes and a fine Brussels carpet covering the floor, and which muffled the sound of Stirling Kincaid's boot-heels as he made his way across to the sideboard to pour a whiskey for his Wednesday night guest.

With his long strong face glinting in the lamplight, Stirling Kincaid blended as perfectly with the splendid room as any piece of expensive furniture. Beyond this house the rancher might well be regarded as immoral, feared and even dangerous by many. Yet here he was the polished host and the very embodiment of a wealthy cattle king taking his ease.

'Water or straight, Brett?' he asked his guest.

Standing by the biggest window watching the purple dusk close in over Silver Dollar's vast green expanses, Brett Cody murmured absently, 'Straight, I guess, Stirling.'

'Yes, I believe that is how you need it tonight,' Kincaid replied, crossing the room with the glasses. He passed the other his drink, studied him quizzically. 'What's wrong?'

'Well, nothing that I reckon you'd want to hear about, Stirling'. Cody lifted his glass. 'Your health.'

'Health,' Kincaid murmured, but didn't drink. He studied the younger man closely, noting the tight lines about the mouth and eyes.

'Better tell me what's eating you, Brett. What is it? Money troubles still?'

Cody smiled wryly. 'You know me too well, Stirling.'

'Ah, thought as much.' Kincaid didn't sound surprised, for he well understood that Cody with his vanity and high-living ways was no businessman. Yet oddly enough, these shortcomings did not disturb Stirling Kincaid. All that really signified for him was that Cody had the name, breeding and class that qualified him to wed his sister and produce the heir or heirs who would one day inherit Silver Dollar Ranch.

'Better tell me about it, Brett,' he suggested, gesturing at a chair.

Cody remained standing. 'Ah, same old thing, Stirling . . . but I don't suppose you could help me to pay some of my—'

'We've been over that before,' Kincaid cut him off in a characteristically brusque way. 'I could loan you money, but I won't and you know why. When you and Barbara are married you will get all the assistance you require, but not before.'

'Sure . . . sure, Stirling. By the way, where is Barbara?'

Kincaid smiled, the genial host once more. 'I'll go find her. Now sit down and take your ease, Brett. Help yourself to another drink.'

Kincaid's geniality vanished as he quit the room, closing the oak-panelled door in back of him. 'Jessie!' he shouted and a maid appeared immediately from one of the doorways opening on to the long corridor which led to the rear of the house. 'Where the hell is Miss Barbara?'

'She said to tell you she is not coming to supper, Mr Kincaid,' the maid replied, looking nervous.

'What? But Mr Cody is here.'

'I think she knows that, Mr Kincaid.'

Kincaid made to retort, changed his mind and made for the stairs leading to the upper floor. Moments later he was rapping on his sister's door. Hard.

'Barbara!' he called. 'What's this nonsense about you not coming to dinner?'

The door opened and his sister stood there, still attired in riding breeches and check shirt.

'Oh . . . Stirling,' she said, passing a hand across her forehead. 'I'm sorry, I just don't feel well tonight.'

Entering the room Kincaid stared hard at his sister. To his eye she appeared as healthy as ever. It did not escape his notice that she avoided his gaze as she crossed the room to sit in the bay window which stood open to the cool evening air.

'Barbara—' he began, but she interrupted.

'Please, Stirling, I don't feel up to arguing.'

His face hardened. 'There won't be any arguments – providing you dress immediately and come downstairs.'

'I refuse to come down. I told you I'm not up to it.'

Kincaid crossed the room to stand over the girl, hard blue eyes glittering. 'I simply don't believe that,' he said tightly. 'You have been acting strangely around Brett lately and I demand to know why.'

'There is nothing. I simply don't feel—'

'You've already told me that and I still don't believe you.'

'Believe whatever you wish, Stirling.'

Stirling Kincaid was unaccustomed to this attitude and felt his control was being challenged. 'All right, let's have this out here and now. You know my feelings towards you and Brett. I always expected that—'

'I know only too well what you expect, Stirling,' she cut him off. 'I've heard it often enough, God knows!'

'Then you'll hear it again. I want you two married and I want an heir to the ranch. I'm fifteen years your senior and I drink too much brandy . . . and I'm certainly not going to see all I've built pass into other hands when I die.'

'Oh, nonsense, Stirling. You'll live another forty years.'

'I could get thrown off my horse and break my neck tomorrow, so you must—'

'Oh, for heaven's sake, if you're so perturbed about all this why don't you marry again and sire a dozen sons?'

'You know why, damnit!'

The girl bit her lip and fell silent. For what he said was true. Her brother's doomed year-long marriage to a socialite from the East had failed officially due to 'irreconcilable differences'. Yet she knew that during that brief union which had produced no offspring, extensive tests in Chicago revealed Stirling was unable to sire children.

So it was up to her to become the brood mare of the Kincaid line . . . or at least that was how it was seen through her brother's eyes.

The silence lasted until the man suddenly swore and strode across to the door. 'Are you coming or not?' he barked.

'No.'

He seemed about to leave, but instead swung back and crossed to her as she rose from the chair to seize her by both shoulders. His face was tight, blue eyes boring into her own.

'It's Ashton, isn't it?' he accused. 'No, don't try to deny it. I've seen the change come over you ever since that bastard came back to town.'

'Stirling, you're hurting me!'

'It's him. Admit it. Come on, I know you too well not to know that—'

'All right!' she blazed. 'Perhaps it is Cord. But you have nothing to worry about, my precious brother, for he would never marry me.'

Kincaid's hands dropped to his sides, the muscles of his lean jawline writhing.

'So,' he breathed. 'I didn't want to believe it . . . but my hunch about you and that badgepacker was right all along. Now I know for sure why he came back after quitting the way he did before. It's you!'

The girl's shoulders slumped and she turned away, infinitely weary now. 'Please, Stirling, leave me be. I don't want to talk about it any more.'

Stirling Kincaid stood staring at his sister in total silence for a long moment before going out at a lunging walk, shaking the great house end to end as he smashed the heavy door shut behind him.

'Ashton?' Brett Cody echoed disbelievingly as Kincaid paced the carpet before him like an enraged animal. 'I don't believe it!'

'You had better believe it, mister,' Kincaid hissed, driving a fist into his palm with a smack. 'Damnation, I will never ignore a hunch after this. I suspected when that son-of-a-bitch badgepacker was in town the last time that he and Barbara were getting too interested in one another but I never thought—'

'If you suspected that why didn't you tell me?' Cody's eyes were filled with jealousy. 'I had the right to know.'

'It was only a hunch back then.' Kincaid stopped pacing to splash liquor into a crystal glass. He tossed it down his throat with a flick of the wrist. When he swung back on Cody his eyes were dangerous. He was by nature a man who could not and would not be thwarted. 'My sister and a tinhorn badgepacker!' He shook his head violently. 'No, by Judas, not while I'm breathing – that will never happen!'

'Never mind you. She's mine and I'm going to have her. Maybe I should see that badgepacker and ram it home – with a gun, if I must.'

Suddenly Kincaid appeared startled, even uncertain. There were times when he treated Cody like a kid, yet he was well aware the man was anything but.

Some of the fury left his face at that and he was suddenly recalling the fact that Cody had spent years being tutored in gunmanship during his college days in the East, that indeed he was the finest pistol shot he'd ever seen.

Momentarily a truly dark scenario flickered through the rich man's mind. He saw Cody bracing the sheriff in a jealous rage then cutting him down . . . end of the Ashton problem! Then reason saw him cast this scenario aside almost immediately.

Too many uncertainties.

Right now he wanted Ashton gone, dead, or whatever. Yet he knew he would never risk his vision and dream of the perfect marriage and its ideal outcome – a future son and heir for himself and the great ranchero with the right bloodlines. . . .

He squared his shoulders, sipped his brandy and concentrated.

Plainly something surely must be done about that lawdog. He wanted the arrogant bastard gone from his town and his life, wanted it fast. But how did you rid yourself of a fast gun badgepacker who plainly now was posing a serious threat to himself and his many goals and ambitions.

Then it hit him with a jolt. 'McCrow!' he said suddenly.

Cody stared. 'What did you say?'

His face suddenly alight with excitement, the rich man snapped his fingers and swiftly crossed the room to Cody. 'McCrow!' he repeated. 'That gunslick from the Twenty Mile who tangled with Ashton just the other night in town!'

Cody, still brooding over Barbara and Cord Ashton, was slow to catch on. 'What are you driving at, Stirling?

Kincaid clapped a hand on his arm, his face strong and commanding. 'This is about as plain as anything can get. That damned slick-shooting badgetoter has to go. He shouldn't even be here, and now this matter with my sister . . . no, there's just one solution. Ashton's got to go!'

'But he wouldn't quit, Stirling.'

'I'm not talking quitting. When I say he's got to go, I'm saying he's got to be put in the ground!' He paused to slam a fist into his palm again, an habitual gesture when excited. 'Ashton kills people who cross him, and by God and by Judas, so will we—'

The statement was slow to register with Cody, yet when it did, his face flushed with a sick kind of excitement.

'All right . . . all right, by God!' He sounded breathless, then was uncertain again. 'But how . . . or maybe the question is – who? If we want Ashton taken down then we—'

'It's not if,' Kincaid cut him off, pacing to and fro. 'It's when and who.' He propped and nodded grimly. 'And now I've set my mind to it, I've got both answers. When? Soon as possible. And who? Why, there's only one answer to that. McCrow!'

Cody's eyes were wide. 'Damn! I never thought of that. Everyone says McCrow can't be beaten. And I saw him gun down Billy Healy that day in town and he sure—'

'Never mind that,' Kincaid broke in. 'It's enough to know McCrow is the best, and I doubt he's ever turned down an easy dollar.'

'Then – then you're really serious about setting him after Ashton, Stirling?'

'Why not? He's a killer, we all know that. And that is what we need here. A killer, pure and simple.'

'But—'

'No buts. Look, Brett, right from Ashton coming back to town everybody's been half expecting him and McCrow to clash. All we've got to do is make certain that happens.' He paused and nodded, eyes bright with excitement. 'And I believe McCrow would gun his own mother for a thousand dollars, don't you?'

It was all still going too fast for Cody, yet even so he was beginning to grow excited. Developments that day had cast a shadow over his whole future, yet he could see them fading fast now. He'd even considered, then rejected the jealous notion of bracing Ashton himself, yet whenever he sighted McCrow on the streets he was reminded afresh of the difference between a handy man with a Colt, himself, and a man who made a living with it, the sheriff.

'You'd dare go that far, Stirling?' he said, vastly impressed yet apprehensive. 'But Babs? What if—?'

'Enough jaw,' Kincaid cut in. 'It's got to be done and will be. End of story. All right – I want you to ride out to the Twenty Mile and close the deal. I'll give you half the money to give to McCrow and he'll get the rest when the job is done. Tell him we want Ashton in the ground and we don't care how he goes about it so long as he does it quick.'

Brett Cody nodded eagerly, yet the moment Kincaid disappeared to get the cash money the doubts kicked in. What if McCrow turned them down, then talked? Or worse: if Ashton was to kill the killer? What then? Was it possible the tinstar might figure who was behind the deal and then come after him. . . ?

'Here it is.'

Kincaid was back and pressing wads of notes into his hand.

'Are you sure this is the way to do it, Sterling? I mean, may be we should sit back and think—'

Kincaid paused in his counting, eyes as cold as ice. 'Do you want to marry Barbara and inherit everything I've got, or not?'

'You know I do. . . .'

'Then this is the only way,' Kincaid rapped. And went on pressing money into his hands.

CHAPTER 7

COLD STEEL, HOT LEAD

With her first glance through the landing window it appeared to Kitty Dechine that the couple in her upstairs room were dancing. But if it was a dance it seemed a particularly vigorous one, she thought. Then suddenly furniture was sent slamming into a wall with an impact that rocked the sporting house and Kitty's hand flew to her throat in alarm.

'That's not dancin'!' she screamed, running to bang clenched fists against the door. 'Cut that fightin'! This is a respectable joint, goddamnit!'

She might have saved her breath. For this was serious body contact surging to and fro across the room, with drunken animal grunts coming from ugly Brunk

Tonner mingling with hissing cries of pure fury from Lucy May Gibbs.

'Stop this or I'll call the goddamn law!' threatened Kitty as half-clad girls and gaping clients appeared in doorways behind her. 'Stop it, I say—'

Her voice cut off as Lucy May momentarily broke away from her adversary, and it was only then that Kitty saw the flash of light coming off steel in the girl's right hand.

'Holy Mother!' she cried, backing away. 'They're going to do it properly this time. She's got a knife – they'll kill one another!'

'Who is it, Kitty?' a voice hollered from along the hallway.

'Brunk and Lucy May!' Kitty cried, rushing for the stairs. 'Who else?'

Who else indeed? For the 'romance' between the bordello's ugliest client in beetle-browed Tonner, a miner from the Rattlesnake Hills, and Kitty's wild half-breed beauty queen had been marked by violence ever since the couple met professionally for the first time a short six weeks earlier. Brunk had taken his first look at Lucy May, fell in love on the spot, and a bare half hour later threw her down the stairs.

Instinct warned the fiesty madam that simple violence would not satisfy Brunk's primitive urges today, and she was out on the street in a flash screaming for the law or passers-by – anybody stupid enough to respond and try to prevent a possible killing which could result in her place being shut down by the law. Again.

Passers-by paused to watch, always interested in anything which promised to provide excitement on a blustery Saturday afternoon.

'What's goin' on up there, Kitty?' laughed a Twenty Mile cowboy. 'You get caught out over-chargin' your customers again?'

Her hand gesture was obscene as she filled her lungs and bellowed, 'Sheriff! Where is that goddamn sheriff when a body needs him?'

'I'm here, Miss Dechine,' said a familiar voice and the tall figure of Ashton came pushing through the swelling crowd. 'What is it?'

'Upstairs, Sheriff!' Kitty gasped, pointing. 'Lucy May has a knife and—'

Not waiting to hear more Ashton strode inside to take the stairs two at a time, Kitty puffing behind him and leaving an ever-swelling crowd of curious spectators behind her below.

Shouldering his way through the crowd of girls and paying customers now choking the upstairs corridor, Ashton took one quick look through the window, saw the struggling figures and didn't hesitate. His shoulder hit the locked door hard. There was a splintering crash and the door burst open and he strode in.

Brunk Tonner, runty and mean, lay gasping amongst the ruins of a chair against the bed. His shirt was slashed and there was blood on him and across the floor. Standing panting in the centre of the room, knife in hand and her flimsy robe gaping open, Lucy May Gibbs made a formidable sight even for a veteran town-tamer.

'All right, Lucy May,' Ashton said quietly, extending a hand. 'I'll have the knife.'

'Take it off me if you're man enough, Ashton,' she hissed. 'I'll split you crotch to Christmas if you try it.'

'Give the man the goddamn knife, you dumb bitch!' Kitty screeched from the doorway.

'Butt out, you broken down old harlot!' was Lucy's snappy response.

She was distracted for just that moment. That was all Ashton needed. A gunfighter's lightning reflexes were revealed in that swift lunge that took him to the woman, his hand clamping over her wrist. She shrieked and raked at his face with red nails, but Kitty was faster, darting into the fray and connecting with Lucy May's jaw with as nifty an elbow jolt to the jaw as the lawman had witnessed in weeks.

Lucy May was down and nearly out.

Cord was grinning as he emerged from the fray, thinking it was over. Maybe everyone felt that way, with just the one exception. Despite bleeding slashes on arms and shoulders from Lucy May's fury, Brunk Tonner was suddenly playing the role of gentleman and a knight errant as he bawled, 'You think it's funny my woman getting cold-decked, you tin-star dudemaster!'

And charged.

Ashton sidestepped and his Colt appeared as if by magic in his fist as the Cousin Jack's momentum carried him close. He swung the piece with a force that belted Tonner halfway out the door, scattering Kitty and a clutch of her screaming girls in wild confusion.

Tonner hit the floor out cold and Lucy May scrambled up, screaming. 'You've killed him, you dirty bastard! You've killed the man I love!'

Ashton didn't even blink as he housed his piece. His working life was studded with situations exactly like this: he'd learned a lot early in his career about strange love in odd places.

'He's not dead, Lucy,' he reassured. 'But one or both of you soon might be if you two love birds don't learn to get along a little better.'

A girl sniggered, and across the room someone else began to laugh. But Kitty Dechine was not smiling as the peace officer headed for the door.

'Sheriff Ashton! Aren't you going to arrest anybody?'

He shook his head. 'Have some of the boys tote Tonner up to Doc Claybank's, Kitty. And if you can just quieten Lucy May down some she'll be back at work in an hour or so. No real harm done.'

'Well, that's some fine lawman, I must say,' Kitty Dechine said in disgust as his tall figure disappeared down the stairs. She looked around for support amongst clients and their girls clustered about her. 'Not a lawman's bootlace if you ask me.' This from a woman who'd just been rescued from having her throat slit mere minutes before.

'Lucky for you he's a lawman who knows his job, Kitty,' a mocking voice called from the doorway. Kitty whirled sharply with a hot retort on her lips, yet it died right there. For the man standing in the doorway with a thin black cheroot jutting from his teeth, was Wild Jack Mason.

You didn't argue with lethal Jack. Nobody did.

Emerging on to the street below Ashton paused to confront the crowd still gathered expectantly there. 'All right, folks, show's over. Move along.'

Obediently the mob began breaking up. As the lawman started off in the direction of Federation Street, Mayor Don Garroway and banker Jobe Calvin approached.

'Sheriff,' Garroway said anxiously, 'we just heard there was a killing at Kitty's.'

'Just a ruckus,' Cord reassured. 'Lucy May and Brunk Tonner – again.'

Calvin made to speak, but broke off. Four men had just emerged from Kitty's toting a battered and dazed Tonner. Head lolling and mouth agape, the man appeared to be in far worse shape than was actually the case as they toted him by on their way to the medico's.

'You call that a little ruckus, Sheriff?' Calvin asked edgily.

'Nothing to fret about, Mr Calvin.'

'Disgusting!' Calvin said, glaring across at Kitty's.

'We see incidents like this every week at that place. It should be shut down.'

'I am inclined to agree, Sheriff,' Garroway weighed in.

'Never mistake smoke for fire, gentlemen,' Ashton advised, moving off. 'If the Kitty Dechines were all we had to fret about here we'd be in far better shape than is the case.'

As he continued on to Federation, the lawman doubted that Calvin and Garroway would share his views, yet he knew he was right. This was the frontier. Drunken brawls, cowboys shooting out street lamps and eruptions of violence in sporting houses and suchlike were all part of life in places like Sugar Creek.

They posed little threat either to the towns or to men like himself. That real danger rested with the mobs, the drygulchers, or gunners as lethal as Kell McCrow.

He reached the corner of Federation and Kiowa and paused to finger his hat back and surveyed the wide avenue. Saturday afternoon, and Sugar Creek was crowded with towners, cowboys and miners and their families. So far it was tolerably quiet apart from the dust-up at Kitty's. And yet again he was aware of that air of brooding expectancy along the street, though this time sensed he might be able to guess at the cause of it.

The smart money was saying that if Kell McCrow intended coming to town sooner rather than later, he would likely make it a Saturday. But so far, nary a sign.

He moved on with honest folks and the other kind alike all making way for him.

He had a hunch McCrow could show yet didn't allow that to faze him. In his line of work there was always a McCrow or maybe a dozen of his kind a man must watch out for. It went with the territory. His experience was that nine times out of ten the bad trouble folks anticipated rarely happened.

In any case, the ones he felt he had to watch here were not gunslingers or brawlers but rather men with vast kingdoms of grass and cattle along with the bankers, the wheeler-dealers. Plus, of course, all those others who hated him for one reason or another.

He was keenly aware of Stirling Kincaid and what he represented.

Somehow he'd expected to clash with Kincaid by this. Town-tamer and cattle baron had been enemies from day one, and now the word was out that Kincaid suspected that Ashton's return might have something to do with his sister, which Cord could hardly deny. He'd picked up enough local gossip to realize Kincaid was desperate for the wedding between Barbara and Brett Cody to be announced, yet this still hadn't happened.

But how might he react if and when it was?

He forced a grin. 'Play the cards as they are dealt, Cord,' he warned himself. There was more than enough to occupy him here in curbing the wilder elements and being constantly at the ready whenever trouble erupted. He was already receiving respect and appreciation from the solid citizenry, and this was always encouraging. But always in the background was an awareness of those dangerous men who'd considered him gone for good, only to return with badge and gun.

How and when they might react was anybody's guess. Yet neither they nor Barbara were permitted to intrude on his thoughts in the hour he spent covering the crowded town before heading on back for the jailhouse. He was the lawman at work and this place was once again learning to know that and feel it.

Yet time passed uneventfully and he was finally thinking of coffee and maybe a half-hour's relaxation with his boots up on the desk, when he sighted the surrey tied up at the far end of the jailhouse gallery.

He stopped on sighting the Silver Dollar brand on the horse's rump and next moment Barbara Kincaid appeared framed in the jailhouse doorway.

'Good afternoon, Sheriff Ashton,' she said with mock formality. Then she smiled. 'I wish to lodge a complaint.

'Barbara—' His throat felt dry; she looked so lovely. Then, quickly he drew off his hat. 'It's fine to see you. So . . . what might this complaint of yours be?'

She moved to stand directly before him. She wore

a pair of men's Levis with a simple open-necked white shirt. She was dagger slim and vibrantly alive as she reached out to touch his hand.

'I'm complaining bitterly because I've been neglected by a gentleman who hasn't contacted me in almost a week. Do you think you can do anything about that unsatisfactory situation, Sheriff?'

For a moment Ashton's face remained expressionless. Challenged by the pressures and tensions of his new job, he'd tried all week to keep this woman out of his thoughts. Yet just looking at her now made him realize how completely he'd failed.

Then abruptly the tightness left his features and he was smiling. 'Why, I believe I just might be in a position to do something at least, Miss Kincaid. Would you care to step into my office and swear out a formal complaint about being neglected?'

Kell McCrow rode for Sugar Creek.

The gunman was relaxed in his saddle as the horse carried him through the blustery Saturday afternoon while he watched low clouds tugging their shadows behind them across the rangelands.

A cigarette clamped between his teeth trailed smoke over one shoulder and he was reckoning that this day would likely prove to be big, maybe even the biggest of his life.

The old familiar thrill went through him as he adjusted his sky-blue bandanna then raised his hand to pat the thick comfortable wad made by the five hundred dollars nestling in his shirt pocket.

'No maybe about it,' he corrected himself out loud, causing the horse to toggle its ears. 'Today will be the big day. . . .'

He gazed at the sky and felt a swift sureness run though him. He was ready. Ashton's unheralded return had taken him off guard last week. He was never at his best at such times, but rather liked to think long and carefully about a situation and slowly build himself up to achieve that edge of razor-sharp readiness before going into action.

Only then did he know he was invincible.

He was smiling as he forded a little willow-fringed creek, reflecting both on the money and Brett Cody.

Cody had surprised him when he came to visit him out at Twenty Mile two nights before with the offer of a gun job and the fat wad of cash to make it interesting.

Cody wanted Ashton blown away for some reason of his own and had produced hard cash as an incentive.

The irony in this still tickled the killer, a man certainly not known for his sense of humour. For the reality was that sooner or later he might well have buckled on his shooters and gone after Ashton anyway for reasons both men were aware of.

Gunslinger and town-tamer went back to Ashton's earlier tenure here and they'd clashed repeatedly then. After Ashton quit town McCrow might have risen to top gun in a half wild town but for the one exception. Wild Jack Mason had also cut more notches which included several big names. Yet thus far the two guntippers had got along well enough to prevent their rivalry becoming deadly.

But McCrow's history with Ashton was a very different one – volatile and loaded with enmity on both sides. Indeed, ever since Ashton's recent return McCrow had been readying himself to come back to town to call the badgeman out, and then a client had turned up at his door offering big money for him to take the lawman down.

It was like destiny was playing this hand, with Ashton the certain loser!

It was exciting yet McCrow kept cautioning himself as he started out, for such a Colt showdown would surely be no pushover – but before that ride was through all the gunman's caution had faded until again he was sincerely rating himself the faster man.

He inhaled the afternoon fragrances of the open rangeland and saw the future clearly. This victory would see him resume his standing as one of the two top gunslingers within a hundred miles along with Wild Jack Mason and nobody would ever again get to post him out of any town again as Ashton had done.

With Ashton gone he would again be in high demand in the gun trade. There wouldn't be a man who'd fail to tip his hat to him on the street, a kid who didn't know his name. He could even envision Wild Jack Mason going out of his way to buy him a drink and treating him like an equal.

Kell McCrow, gun king!

He moved his horse into a faster lope, eager to get there now.

Five in the afternoon with the wind blowing in from across the cattle lands to bring a duster that filled the sky above the town with a strange yellow light as Sheriff Cord Ashton drove Barbara Kincaid from the jailhouse to the American House Hotel.

Ignoring the stares and whispers as they drew up the sheriff handed the young woman down and flipped a coin to a kid to take the rig around back.

The couple entered the hotel together.

Barbara was already booked into the hotel for the night. There was a church social to be held in the evening which she would attend with her friend, Bess Fletcher.

Ashton collected the key from the desk clerk and handed it to her with a sober nod. 'Well, I'd better get back on to the street.' He gave a mock grimace. 'Saturday night, you know? And the boys can get restless.'

'Can't you come up just for a few minutes, Cord?'

The clerk coughed. Ashton chilled him with a stare then turned back to her.

'Folks mightn't think that proper, Barbara,' he heard himself say. 'You know how people talk.'

'Well,' she smiled, 'if the sheriff is so concerned about the old biddy gossips then let's sit over there in the lobby . . . just for a few minutes.'

There was no way he could refuse. They had been together an hour and it had seemed more like a minute. They'd talked casually and easily like old friends without once touching on deeper things, such as their time together here as lovers before he'd allowed pressure from her family and the demands of his profession to convince him to quit and leave town.

He'd stayed away. But maybe he'd always known he would eventually return. He'd have never come back had she married; he still didn't know why she hadn't done so. But a combination of Sugar Creek's slide back into its old violent ways coupled with the fact she had remained single had proven more than enough incentive for him to accept the council's contract to take over at the jailhouse.

He knew of no law against any of that.

'Do you think you might call in at the dance tonight?' she asked, when they were seated beneath a window.

He didn't answer immediately. A man had just walked by outside. He'd never seen him before but knew his breed. Gunslick, hardcase – maybe even outlaw. There was no way a lawman could feel easy about the way this place was heading until it was reined in to where he'd had it once before.

'If I get time . . . sure,' he replied. He hesitated a moment, then asked, 'Will Brett be there?'

She looked down, serious again. 'Possibly not.'

He didn't want to ask the next question, yet somehow knew he must.

'Nothing wrong, is there, Barbara? You two, I mean?'

She spread her hands. 'I just don't know. We . . . we haven't been getting on very well lately.'

'Any particular reason?'

She glanced up, her expression sober. After a moment she said, 'Perhaps it's you, Cord.'

'Me?' He sounded surprised, but wasn't. He'd known from the start that his return would affect a lot of people, likely nobody more so than this woman and the man she planned to marry.

Yet he felt no guilt. He'd watched Sugar Creek slide downhill over recent months and knew he'd come back as much to look out for this woman's safety as for any other reason.

He would stay until certain of her safety again. Unless, of course, she wanted it otherwise.

He was on the verge of asking her that loaded question when she glanced at her watch and rose in that quick way she had.

'Late already.' She made a grimace. 'You will stop by at the dance?'

'Sure.'

She held out her hand. 'Until tonight.'

'Tonight.'

He watched her cross the lobby and mount the stairs. He stood there long after she'd vanished before realizing folks were staring. By the time he'd put on his hat and walked out he was the town-tamer again, sober and almost sombre as he paused to glance both ways along Federation Street before striding off to check out the saloons.

As he shouldered through the batwings of the Prairie Flower Saloon, a solitary horseman swung into sight at the far end of Federation, the last rays of afternoon sun glinting off the poker chip holding his blue bandanna in place at his throat.

CHAPTER 8

GUNS AND GOODBYE

'No more for you, Mick,' the lawman warned the drunken miner lolling untidily across the billiard table at the Prairie Flower Saloon. 'You've had enough.'

'Just one more, Sheriff?' pleaded thirsty Mick Tuft.

'I said no. Last Monday you had "just one more" and you wound up in jail for brawling. That's not going to happen again tonight.'

A massive sigh. 'Whatever you say, Sheriff.'

As the lawman turned away from the table, saloon-keeper Glede Skelley called to him from the bar. 'A glass before you go, Sheriff?'

'Maybe later, Mr Skelley,' Ashton replied, crossing to join him. He rested an elbow on the zinc edge and turned to survey the room. 'Brisk trade tonight.'

'Like they say . . . everybody and his brother.' The man leaned towards him and added, 'Yessir, business booming all over, thanks to you, Sheriff.'

'How is that?'

'Well, mostly when men come into town now they're more interested in drinkin' than fightin'. That's good for business and costs me a heap less in repairs. Sure you won't have that shot?'

'Well, maybe just one.'

He realized he needed the drink the moment he took his first taste with one ear cocked to the barman's chatter and the other attuned to the sounds of the room. The atmosphere seemed about right yet he was still aware of that vague undercurrent which could hint at budding trouble. But he took another mouthful of the smooth liquor and began to relax, allowing himself to think about Barbara across at the American House Hotel – possibly right at this minute preparing to leave for the dance and looking a million dollars.

He abruptly straightened and set his shot glass down as he swung to face the batwing doors.

'What is it, Sheriff?' Skelley asked nervously.

The lawman didn't reply. Yet he knew he'd detected a subtle change in the murmuring hum of the voices that might only be picked up by a practised ear. The saloon was still rowdy yet instinct told him that it was as if it was Federation Street that had suddenly fallen quieter outside.

How come?

He set his glass down and made for the batwings. He was halfway there when Lon Green came rushing in, long hair flopping across his brow. The boy's eyes widened on sighting him, and he yelled, 'Cord! He's here!'

Silence engulfed the crowded bar room with every eye focusing on the two as they came together before the doors.

'McCrow?' Ashton guessed.

'Yeah, Cord. He's down by B.B. Corral.'

A long moment's silence slowly gave way to the sounds of exhalations of held breath coming from the crowd around the two men, with every eye now fixed upon the sheriff.

All Sugar Creek knew he'd posted the gunfighter from town along with several others of his kind.

'I barred him for a certain period that hasn't been exhausted, so by showing up he stands in contempt of the authority invested in me by the city council,' Cord stated in a level voice that carried. 'I'll arrest him and deal with any man who attempts to interfere.'

He headed for the batwings.

'Cord!' Lon said urgently. 'Let me come—'

'Stay where you are!' Ashton rapped, then placed both hands atop the half doors and stepped outside.

From the porch he surveyed Federation Street in the early night. Minutes earlier the street had been crowded, now less than a dozen men were to be sighted on the walks. The sun was gone but there was still light. The ungreased squawk of a wagon axle sounded stridently loud as a freighter rumbled across the intersection making for the stockyards.

The sheriff started off south walking down the middle of the road and almost immediately sighted McCrow.

The man had appeared abruptly upon the wide plank landing of the Feed and Grain barn. Nobody actually saw him emerge. One moment the gloomy doorway of the barn stood empty, the next the gunfighter was there in striped pants with his big head turning left to right, like a dog hunting a scent.

McCrow went completely still as Ashton came into full sight at a steady walk.

The gunslinger eased away from the barn building and began strolling towards the lawman, his step lithe and easy with rowelled spurs raising a soft chinking sound in the dust. If the man was edgy it did not show. From a distance he resembled a lithe-bodied cowboy maybe out for a good night's fun. It was only up close that the glittering black eyes were seen to burn with deadly intent.

The whole scene was familiar to Cord Ashton. Too familiar. The empty street, the expectant hush, the staring faces and the man with the fast gun who was too proud, too stubborn or just too damned stupid to understand it did not have to be this way.

The lawman drew strength from the fact that he had featured large in more grim scenes like this than he cared to remember, and yet had every time walked away.

A rising breeze flapped the full sleeves of McCrow's blue shirt and he was grinning now.

'That sheriff oughta watch his step,' croaked a red-faced drinker over at the Easy Rider. 'McCrow was laffin' just like that the night he blasted our last sheriff into eternity, b'God!'

Ashton abruptly halted and brushed back the panel of his coat to reveal the unspoken challenge of his Colt .45.

'Your month isn't up, McCrow!'

Kell McCrow stopped to stand very straight with feet wide-planted.

'I never was much for calendar-readin', Ashton.' His tone was insolent.

'You don't have to die.'

'What is this, lawman? You runnin' short of sand? Well, that is curious, for the last time we talked you was soundin' like the bravest *hombre* 'twixt here and Wichita!'

Ashton's jaw lifted fractionally. 'Shuck your gunbelt and submit to arrest or face the consequences!'

'Big words, lawdog . . . nothin' but piss and vinegar. Never mind telling me what you will do! I will kill you where you stand if you don't—'

'Ditch your weapon!'

McCrow hesitated fractionally then sent his right hand slashing down. Ashton's Colt came out in a blur and crashed volcanically in the hush. He triggered twice but the second shot came so close on the heels of the first it sounded like one long explosion of sound, and there would be those later who would argue that but a single bullet was fired.

For a moment neither man moved. Then Kell McCrow took one slow step forward and fell face down in the dust, shot twice through the chest.

Ashton calmly refilled his piece. He didn't go forward to examine the body. He knew where his lead had gone.

When he turned at last to make his way back up the slight slope the whole day seemed suddenly hushed and sucked empty of all sound. When he shouldered through the batwings of the Hard Luck, drinkers scattered, wide-eyed and fearful now.

'A glass of whiskey, barkeep!' he said, his voice sounding unnaturally loud in the silence.

'Yessir, Sheriff Ashton,' said Harry Boon, who just minutes earlier had been loudly predicting Kell McCrow would blast the lawman into eternity. His hands shook as he poured. 'You . . . you all right, Sheriff Ashton?'

'Just the whiskey . . . never mind the jaw!'

'Whatever you say, Sheriff.'

It was just after midnight when Barbara Kincaid saw Lon Green enter the hall, looking about for her. She threaded her way through the dancers to join him by the doors.

He read the question in her eyes, and said, 'He's over at the jailhouse now, Barbara.'

'Is he all right?' She'd not seen Ashton since the shooting although she had searched for him for an hour before the last dance began. She had then seconded Lon to keep an eye out for him.

'I guess so,' replied Green, looking pale and drawn. 'I asked him where he went after the . . . after the gunfight, but he didn't answer. I reckon he's just been off by himself someplace. Maybe we could understand why he might want to do that.'

'Yes, I believe I do. Will you escort me up to the jailhouse, Lon?'

'Sure.'

'Thank you. I'll get my coat.'

Five minutes later they were standing upon the high jailhouse porch where chinks of light showed behind drawn shutters. 'You want me to come in with you, Barbara?' Green asked.

'No thanks, Lon, I'd rather see him alone.' She squeezed the boy's hand. 'But thanks anyway.'

Green nodded and moved off slowly, glancing back over one shoulder. Barbara approached the door and knocked hesitantly. No answer.

'Cord?'

She heard the scrape of a chair, then Ashton's voice. 'Barbara?'

'Yes, it's me.'

After a silence came the sound of a bolt being drawn, the door swung open and Ashton stood before her looking gaunt and pale in the lamplight.

'What is it?' His voice was flat.

'May I come in?'

'I don't feel much like—'

'Please, Cord.'

Ashton hesitated a moment then shrugged and stepped aside for her to enter. He closed the door to blot out the street and motioned to a chair, then went behind the desk and sat. He leaned back with his face thrown into shadow by the heavy lampshade.

'What is it, Barbara?'

'I just had to see if you were all right.'

'I'm fine.'

Her heart went out to him as she studied his face. She knew how he felt. There were those people – her brother amongst them – who said that Cord Ashton was a killer no better than the hellions he was hired to control. Yet she knew he never used his gun if there was another way – only when men like Kell McCrow held the name of law and order to mockery.

She moved her chair closer to the desk and leant her elbows upon it with the lamplight striking highlights from dark tresses.

'Talk to me, Cord. It's always better to talk.'

'What's to say? I killed a man.' A pause, then, 'Another man.'

'You are not to think like that. You know very well there was no other way.'

'Somehow there never is with the McCrows of the world.' His eyes flicked at her. 'Did you see it?'

'No. Is it true that he was carrying a large sum of money on his person?'

Coming out of himself a little now, Ashton nodded. 'He was carrying five hundred dollars. In fifties.'

'I heard that at the dance. Everybody is wondering where a man like that would get such an amount. What do you make of it?'

Ashton frowned as he leant forward to take a cigar from his silver case. 'I'm not sure. But I guess it looks pretty much like he was hired to come against me. And yet I doubt if that would have been necessary in the long term. I believe McCrow would have called me out eventually of his own accord. He was a hard hater.'

'Who would hire him to do something like that . . . if indeed he was hired?

His smile was humourless. 'I'm never short of enemies, Barbara. Matter of fact, you could say I seem to collect them.'

'Please, Cord, let's put it all out of our minds now. It's over, you're alive and we still have a lawman in Sugar Creek. That is all that matters.'

Ashton studied her for a moment then shook his head. 'You're a very unusual girl, Barbara. I guess you always were.'

'In what way?'

'Being here . . . just coming here this way after what happened. You should be horrified, disgusted.'

'I was both when Sheriff Barney Tobin was shot

down, Cord,' she said with spirit. 'And I've certainly been that way when others have lost their lives needlessly. Yet all I feel about what happened this afternoon, is pride. I feel proud there is somebody who won't simply stand back and watch the gunmen and killers take over.'

'Obliged.' It was all he could say but he deeply appreciated the words nonetheless.

Their eyes met and held through a long moment's silence. Ashton appeared to be about to say something further then changed his mind. Hesitantly the girl leaned forward to touch his hand.

'Cord—'

He drew his hand back. 'Don't, Barbara.'

She looked hurt. 'You don't like me to touch you?'

Ashton lunged to his feet. 'Damnit, I want you to more than—' He broke off, expression haggard now. 'Barbara, surely you understand what I'm trying to say? There's no point in us seeing one another because—'

'Because why, Cord? I never really understood why we broke up in the first place.'

'Because I'm a goddman town-tamer,' he said harshly, moving about the room. 'I live by this gun and I'll die by it one day, while you're young with the world at your feet. Now do you understand?'

She didn't reply. Instead she rose and came around the desk, hesitated a moment, then slipped an arm about his waist. There was still uncertainty in him as he stared down at her, yet next moment their lips were meeting.

In that brief span of time the street, the town and a thing called duty ceased to have any meaning – all banished from this quiet room where the night air pressed cold against the window panes.

Then Barbara was saying over and over, 'Cord, I love you . . . I always did. . . .'

'Don't say that. There's only pain that way. For both of us.'

'If I don't say it then I shall always go on thinking it,' she defied him. She moved out of the embrace and brushed back a stray wisp of dark hair, forcing a smile. 'And I have just decreed myself in charge of us. . . .' A pause, then, 'So, life goes on. Now, Cord Ashton, you are going to walk me home, and tomorrow morning you will drive me out to the ranch.'

He stared at her wonderingly. 'I will?' After a long moment, he almost grinned. Suddenly he felt he was all through fighting. At least for tonight.

'Yes, you are. I know you never liked my ordering you around, but you are just going to have to get used to it all over again. So, please get your hat, Mr Ashton.'

They strolled along Federation arm in arm for the hotel, the lawman tall in his dark suit with the loveliest girl in Ramrod Valley at his side. The street lights were shining, the wind felt clean, and it seemed to Cord Ashton he had never seen stars so bright. But for how long they might glitter there was no telling . . . not in this town.

*

Sunday morning's sunlight spilled in through the big bay windows and glowed richly upon the red Brussels carpet and highly polished dining-table, sparkling amber in the glass of whiskey in Stirling Kincaid's big fist.

Kincaid rarely drank or smoked to excess yet throughout the long night just past he had done plenty of both. As a result his morning temper was even worse than usual, as the maid discovered when she came in to enquire innocently if breakfast was required.

'Get the hell out, damn you!' he yelled. The girl vanished and the whiskey glass smashed into fragments against the door as it closed behind her.

The rancher lunged to his feet and crossed to the bureau to pour himself another. He flinched from the bright bars of sunlight angling through the window and drew the back of his hand across an unshaven jaw. 'Five hundred bucks down the drain,' he muttered, kicking a foostool out of his path. 'Five hundred – and now Ashton standing taller than ever. . . .'

He dropped into a chair, took another pull and stared at nothing. The newspaper at his side held a full account of Kell McCrow's bloody demise in Sugar Creek. For some reason Kincaid had hoped the whole thing might appear brighter by daylight, but if anything it looked worse.

He was still hunched in that same position when he heard steps on the gallery outside and then his ramrod's voice; 'Miss Barbara's coming in, Mr Kincaid!'

'Don't bother me, Jubal!'

'Ashton's with her.'

'What?'

The cattle king came out of his chair in a bound to cross the room. As he gained the wide gallery the surrey was just swinging in beneath the ranch yard's title gate. His sister was perched elegantly upon the black leather cushions and at her side, driving, the sheriff of Sugar Creek.

Something sick crossed the watcher's face as the surrey rolled to a halt at the steps.

Barbara's smile turned a little apprehensive as she stepped down. 'Now, Stirling,' she cautioned, 'before you say anything, let me—'

'Get inside!' Kincaid hissed, lunging down the steps. 'I'll deal with you later!'

'I said it wouldn't be a good idea for me to drive you right to home, Barbara,' Ashton remarked as he looped the reins around the whip socket.

'You drove me in because I asked you to,' the girl stated defiantly, matching stare for stare with her brother. 'Now, Stirling—'

'I warned you to shut your mouth!' Kincaid raged, eyes flaring as the lawman stepped down on the opposite side of the rig.

'Don't speak to your sister that way,' Ashton said

with a clear note of warning in his tone as he moved to the rear of the rig where his horse was tethered.

With great effort, Stirling Kincaid managed to throttle his anger back a notch.

'All damned right!' he said through locked teeth. 'If I speak politely enough, Barbara, you might be good enough to answer me how come you went off to that damned dance last night, and now turn up late in the middle of the morning in the company of a low killer?'

'I insisted Cord drive me out,' she replied calmly. 'I did so because I wanted him to and also because I'm heartily sick of the way you carry on about him every time his name arises. You don't seem to understand, Stirling, that I'm entitled to have my friends and also to have them here, if and when I wish.'

His eyes flared yellow. Despite his status and natural authority, the rancher had never managed to bend his equally strong-minded young sister to his will. He knew by the set of her jawline now that she would contest him all the way should he choose to fight. But suddenly he didn't want that. Not now.

'You've made your point,' he conceded thickly. He paused to suck in a big breath. 'Very well. You invited this man to escort you home, and he's done it. Now will you excuse us, sister dear? I want to confer with the sheriff in private.'

Barbara studied him uneasily before turning to Ashton, who said, 'I doubt we have anything to discuss, Kincaid.'

'I'll be the judge of that!' Kincaid spun on his heel. 'We'll talk in the front room. Barbara, you can go upstairs and change or do whatever you have to do.'

'It might not be wise for you to go inside, Cord,' the girl warned as her brother vanished inside. 'I've rarely seen him this angry and I can tell he's been drinking.'

Ashton shrugged. 'I'll talk to him,' he decided. 'Maybe we can clear the air.'

'Very well, if you insist. But I still believe it will be a waste of time.'

'Maybe,' he murmured, and they entered the house together.

'So you did it, gunslinger!' the cattle king accused when Cord entered the vast room. 'You got to carve another notch on that fancy gun of yours . . . in the name of law and order, of course.'

Ashton halted in the centre of the room and met his stare levelly.

'I killed McCrow,' he stated flatly. 'You already know that. So what's to discuss?'

Kincaid strode past him to kick the heavy door shut with a crash that rattled the rafters, whirled to face him again.

'My sister, gunman,' he hissed. 'What else would I want to talk about with the likes of you?'

'You're jumping to conclusions. Barbara asked me to escort her home. Nothing more to it than that.'

'Liar!'

'You use that word kind of loose—'

His tone held a warning. Kincaid was again intuitive enough to catch the whiff of danger but by this was far too angry to heed it.

'You've had your eye on my sister since the day you first saw her,' he accused. 'And don't try to deny it. I saw it from the very start when you were here before, that her money was the big attraction for you – you and all the other gold-digging sons of bitches like you!'

'I reckon I'll be on my way, Kincaid. Talking to you always was a wasted exercise.'

'And what if I say I'm not finished yet?' The cattleman smacked a fist into his palm. 'You'll go when I say, damnit!'

Tight white lines cut the corners of Ashton's mouth as he turned for the door. He paused when the other shouted, 'Yellow-bellied son of a bitch! Can't even handle an argument, can you, gunslinger. If someone disagrees – shoot then . . . or else run. That's your philosophy, right?'

Ashton flipped his hat and caught it. 'Well, talk,' he said softly. 'But choose your words carefully or I just might ram them down your throat.'

'I'll spell it out very plain. I want you out of my town and to hell and gone away from my sister. Pronto! I told you that on your arrival but obviously it didn't make any impression and I realize now where it was I went wrong. I should have offered you money . . . and now I'm prepared to do just that.'

'Money?' Ashton was genuinely taken aback.

'Sure. You know? The stuff your kind kills for. One thousand dollars. You'll have it in your hand today if you agree to quit Sugar Creek and never return.'

Ashton shook his head slowly. He really had not expected this. Maybe he should have. Yet his response would still have been the same either way.

'I wouldn't take one dime from you for any reason. Know why? Because your money is tainted and always was. When I was here before I ran checks on your operations and saw how you stole and double-crossed when you were poor, and when you got rich you used your money to buy up contracts, votes and men. I deal with scum every day in my job but your kind is the lowest. At least vermin like McCraw had the guts to stand and fight like a man . . . something you never were or ever could be.'

That did it.

Kincaid cursed and hurled a vicious blow to the jaw then missed with a wild overhand right as Ashton went low, bobbed up, and connected with a chopping right hook.

Kincaid skidded back on his heels, slammed into the wall but lurched forward again. He swung wildly once then staggered from a truly brutal punch to the side of the head. His legs buckled and his knees hit the carpet with a thud before he toppled to one side and lay motionless – out to the world.

'Cord!'

He whirled to see Barbara framed in the doorway.

'I'm sorry,' he said, stepping over the motionless

figure. 'He gave me no choice.'

The girl rushed by him to kneel at her brother's side.

'He'll be OK, just knocked out,' Cord assured her.

'Oh, Cord,' she said tearfully, rising. 'I didn't want this to happen though I suppose I should have known better. I was just hoping if I brought you out here and made Stirling realize that I wasn't afraid to be seen with you, then perhaps everything might somehow settle down and be fine. But . . . but. . . .'

He put an arm about her shoulders. He felt bad. He'd always known Kincaid regarded him as just a gunslinger with a badge, but he'd hoped to change that view. No chance of that now. Kincaid desperately wanted his only sister to make a brilliant marriage – to the right man – and in so doing help elevate himself to the heights of power and influence. Town-tamers couldn't compete in that high world.

'See to Mr Kincaid,' he ordered the servants who came rushing into the room. 'Cold water and a sip of brandy should do it.'

He took the girl by the elbow and drew her from the room out on to the long gallery just as Jubal and several hands came trotting across the yard to investigate the uproar.

'It's all right!' he called, raising a hand. 'I had a difference with your boss but he's going to be fine.'

The men propped to glance at Barbara, and when she nodded in affirmation turned away to drift off back to bunkhouses and stables.

Ashton followed her at a distance, glancing off to where his horse stood eating oats from a bucket.

'I'm sorry,' he called. 'I . . . I won't come here again.'

She whirled and came back. 'Oh, Cord, it wasn't your fault . . . I know that.' She placed her hands on his shoulders. 'When shall I see you again? I must see you!' she cried with tears in her eyes.

He still felt badly; a gun battle last night; brawling with her brother today. You could do better, Ashton, you could do a whole lot better. . . .

He vaulted into the saddle and gazed down at her, puzzled, 'You still want to see me after . . . all this. . . ?'

'Yes, Cord, very much.'

'Then I'll be in touch,' he assured, turned the horse with his knees and headed for the trail.

Barbara Kincaid watched him disappear from sight before turning slowly back to the great house.

CHAPTER 9

THE CHALLENGE

Brett Cody said, 'You're not serious, Stirling?'

'Do I look like I'm joking?'

Cody shook his head. He realized his brother-in-law-to-be appeared more grim-faced than he'd ever seen him as they stood under the noon sun at the Bar 50 Ranch several hours later. The entire right side of Kincaid's face was discoloured with angry bruising and he was acting meaner than Cody had ever seen him.

By contrast Cody appeared impressive, as usual. The Eastern-educated sportsman and gentleman of impeccable breeding and background always impressed as exactly the kind of potential son-in-law rich families dreamed of.

But, of course, to complete that perfect picture,

he must also be rich.

Unluckily the Cody family's fortunes had gone downhill fast under Brett's reckless mismanagement and high living. Yet his blue blood credentials remained impeccable. And to Stirling Kincaid this was virtually all that mattered, never more so than right now.

When his sister and Cody eventually got to celebrate their wedding of the decade – which they certainly would – Kincaid planned to merge both ranches then mould them into the finest cattle empire in the territory with him holding the reins and thereby guaranteeing all of the family's great goals would surely be achieved.

So the die was now cast, at least in Kincaid's mind. Cody would marry his sister and the social and economic future of the Kincaid clan would be set in cement. What a vision this was, and yet what a potential disaster that a gunslinger sporting a lawman's star should show up from out of the past to threaten it all!

Yet he knew he could handle even this. He'd surmounted all challenges in his life up until now, with the exception of one. He would correct that swiftly.

And so he talked while the younger man listened until finally forced to interrupt.

'Let me get this straight, Stirling. You're suggesting you and I should team up to get rid of Ashton once and for all? Put him in the ground? Is that really what you're saying?'

'It's not just a plan, it's what has to happen. I might be rich and influential enough to hire professionals to take Ashton down. But that could prove risky, and won't be necessary. For when it's all boiled down he is just another gunslick hiding behind a star . . . and I see him clearly as ready to be taken.'

Cody was alarmed at first, but that was already beginning to fade. For the the younger man had always believed in Kincaid's vast capabilities and his vision for the future for the three of them. This ruthless streak the other was displaying in full now excited him, and he'd never admit it scared him just a little as well.

This situation was bringing out the real Cody. There was violence in his past; his rich parents had bailed him out of serious trouble more than once. He'd always felt a strong kinship with Kincaid and saw the two families' marriage-locked union as his pathway to a future.

But there was one final uncertainty to clear up in his mind. 'You say Babs is really sweet on the sheriff, Stirling? I mean . . . seriously?'

Kincaid looked him straight in the eye. 'If we don't act fast you'll lose her to him. Is that serious enough for you?'

'Judas! I wondered why she's been acting so weird lately!' He stared into space for a long moment and by the time he turned back to Kincaid his whole demeanor had become suddenly grim and resolute. 'All right, count me in. So tell me, how do we go about taking Ashton down?'

*

A mean wind was gusting down Federation Street as Ashton came along the plankwalk. The wind had sprung up just on dusk to send swirls and eddies of dust up against the false-fronts and rattle loose eaves atop the General Store. Now it blew stronger from the south and the lawman held on to his hatbrim as he paused on the Wardlock Street corner before moving on towards the central block.

His tread was heavy as he made his way past a bunch of cowhands loafing out front of the billiard parlour, then circled round a second larger group comprising bearded diggers from the Sister Fan Mine.

The day had been long and his face was still marked up some from the brawl with Kincaid, his eyes gritty with fatigue. Cowhands and miners had been drifting in from the ranches ever since sundown, their presence guaranteeing another busy night ahead. And now this damned wind. . . .

Ashton had trodden the plankwalks of too many frontier towns not to understand the effect weather could have on men's moods, particularly with the breed most inclined to raise hell at times.

On hot and steamy days men were inclined to loaf about and drink and gamble, seldom able to muster the energy for serious trouble. Cold days seemed to have much the same effect, but it was often the rain and wind that seemed to stir the blood and trigger off activity.

With dust blowing thick and trees whipping in the wind some folks seemed to feel they just had to shout and howl at the moon while others might be tempted to go even further than that if there wasn't a restraining hand to reel them in.

This surely was such a night in Sugar Creek and Cord was very conscious of the atmosphere as he paused across from the Paradise Saloon where the piano tinkled tinnily and half the faro layouts were already doing brisk business.

The joint was nearly half-filled and he glimpsed the case-keeper, bulky and check-suited, standing by the stairs puffing on a fat cigar and looking properous and pleased with his simple world of high hopes and dodgy dice.

The man waved a pudgy hand. The lawman nodded soberly and continued on his rounds.

He found Don Garroway breasting the bar of the Prairie Flower Saloon when he arrived. The mayor greeted him with a smile then frowned on noticing the bruises.

'Why, you look a tad the worse for wear, if you don't mind my remarking, Sheriff.'

Ashton leaned one elbow on the bar and surveyed the Prairie Flower which, like the Paradise, was also filling rapidly now. 'I'll survive, Mr Mayor.'

Garroway rubbed the side of his fleshy nose. 'I, er, heard about what took place at the Silver Dollar . . . or maybe you don't want to discuss that?'

'What happened between Kincaid and me has

been brewing ever since I returned. Well, it's over and maybe the air might clear for a spell.'

The mayor digested this, frowned, reached a decision.

'I'll be honest and admit to you that Kincaid has been of increasing concern both to myself and my fellow councillors of late, Sheriff. There have been rumours linking him with violence and several unsavoury incidents . . . even one story hinting at a murder. I must confess I feel that he has developed into a very dangerous and ruthless man.'

'You could be right.'

'Therefore I feel it my duty to warn you about him in the aftermath of the thrashing you handed out. To my recollection nobody's ever whipped him before and I feel he won't simply let it rest there.'

'I appreciate your warning, Mayor.'

'Well, now that's off my chest, buy you a drink, Sheriff Ashton?'

He declined. Today more than ever he felt he might need a clear head on the streets of this town. His town.

A gust of wind buffeted him as he quit the building, yet he found the elements bracing tonight. He lit a cigar and set off on his rounds only to be drawn back quickly by a sudden disturbance over at the general store.

He arrived in time to break up a brawl between the locals and a bunch of roughnecks from the Box 90. He got their story, issued warnings then sent them off muttering and cussing yet unlikely to cause any further trouble, so he believed.

He encountered Lon Green on the street and they walked a block together with their backs to the wind. He didn't realize Lon was steering him back towards his hotel until the youngster stopped before the familiar tall doors.

'You're going up to take a nap, Cord,' he said firmly. 'You're all played out, and no wonder.'

They argued. Sure, he was weary, but with the scent of more trouble in the air, insisted he couldn't quit. The wrangle grew heated yet Lon simply refused to give in. Cord was puzzled by his insistence yet finally realized the man was most likely right. He should face it; deep down, he knew he was beat. And that was no way for a badgeman to operate in a town like this one.

So he went in, collected his keys and mounted the stairs. Slowly. Upon reaching his room he jerked to a halt. The door stood ajar.

He drew his Colt, cocked it then raised his boot and kicked the door fully open.

'Cord?'

Astonishment registered as he found himself confronting Barbara Kincaid.

'Barbara! What the—?'

'I'm sorry I startled you, Cord. The clerk said it would be all right if I came up and waited for you. You're not annoyed, are you?'

'Of course not.' He'd never meant anything more.

He stepped inside, put the gun away and closed the door behind him. 'Just surprised is all. . . .' He paused with a smile. 'Just a minute . . . you saw Lon, didn't you?'

'I'm afraid I did . . . we set this up.'

'Well, I guess I'm glad you did. . . .' He paused to frown. 'But how come?' he asked, taking her by the arm and guiding her to the couch. 'I mean—'

He could see how serious she appeared now. 'I just needed to see you again after what happened at the ranch, had to make sure you were all right.'

'I'm fine. How is your brother?'

'That's largely why I came,' she told him. 'Oh, Stirling recovered quickly enough from the fight, but I've never seen him in such a strange mood . . . frightening almost. Brett came over later and they were locked away talking for a long time before they eventually mounted up and rode off without saying where they were going. I have this feeling they might mean you harm, Cord, I really do.'

He was not surprised to hear this. Not for a moment could he see Kincaid accepting what had happened lying down.

Yet he didn't say as much. 'He'll get over it, you'll see.'

'I doubt it. You see he confronted me and accused me of being in love with you.'

He stared.

'What did you say?'

'I . . . I told him it was true.'

Suddenly Ashton was no longer thinking about Stirling Kincaid, the troubled streets below or even that whiff of trouble on the air. All he could think of was this woman, what she had just said and what it meant to him. And when he held her it seemed both finally realized they could never allow anything to part them again – nothing.

Tears brimmed in her eyes as she whispered, 'Cord . . . my darling Cord. . . .'

It was one hour later when Ashton returned to his room after seeing Barbara off to the Silver Dollar with two cowboy escorts. She had wanted to stay on but he'd insisted she return to the spread. This was without doubt the best night of his life, but even love could not alter harsh reality or the demands of duty. There were still the crowded streets, the nagging possibility of further trouble and, most concerning of all perhaps, this lingering, deep-seated weariness in his bones.

He knew he'd over-extended himself and the need for rest was the factor he must deal with first. With the town crowded and edgy and maybe heading for trouble later on, his one imperative had to be to get in a couple of solid hours' sleep before showing himself upon the streets tonight, and then be prepared to stay there most likely until daybreak.

He recalled stretching out atop the coverlet fully dressed with his mind deliberately blanked to everything other than the sweet taste of her kiss on his lips. . . .

He didn't remember dropping off. It seemed he'd only just closed his eyes before the sudden thud of knuckles on his door jolted him awake.

He sat up and reached for the gun beneath his pillow.

'Who is it?'

'Lon!'

Swinging stockinged feet to the floor he crossed to the door and jerked it open. Lon Green stood blinking in the bright light of the hallway.

'Goddamn . . . what time is it?'

'Just gone ten, Cord. Sorry to rouse you but it's the Box 90 boys.'

He muttered a soft curse yet was rapidly coming fully awake as he drew his boots on then stood erect to strap on the gunbelt. 'What the hell are they up to, Lon? Nothing original, I'll wager.'

'You'd be right. Nah, same old rough-house and ruckus story. Joe Martin just shoved Tad Fuller through a front window.'

'In that case you did the right thing calling me.' He shrugged into his coat and grabbed down his hat as they headed for the door. 'Let's go. You can head on to the jailhouse to make sure we've got an empty cell waiting for Mr Joe Martin!'

The thud of Ashton's six-shooter barrel making contact with the brawler's skull carried clearly across the street from the saloon where two men stood watching from the shadows of a porch.

The pair saw it all when Ashton dropped Martin to his knees with gun butt then stepped back when the wild man made a feeble attempt to seize his legs before slumping face down on the plankboards with blood running from his head, out to the world.

'Judas, Stirling!' Brett Cody said nervously as they watched Martin's companions lift the limp form and head off with him in the direction of the jailhouse. 'Did you see that?' He ran his tongue over dry lips. 'Maybe this wasn't such a great notion after all. . . .'

'What's wrong with you?' Kincaid snapped. 'Back at the Prairie Flower you were ready to take Ashton on one-handed and blindfolded.' He gestured dismissively across the street. 'Anybody could deck a drunk like that.'

'Maybe . . . maybe not. . . .'

Kincaid registered disgust. He knew the whiskey was wearing off with Cody and that the lawman's impressive handling of the drunks was raising grave doubts in the man's mind concerning Ashton's capabilities, should a showdown occur later.

No such doubts affected the boss of Silver Dollar. The violence back at the spread had affected Kincaid and Cody very differently. Kincaid had been shamed by it, stung and finally driven to action. He'd believed he and Ashton were destined to clash ever since the day the lawman hit town, but had needed to experience the real danger the man represented at first hand before he could feel sure he could still take him down. And he was.

The plotters had finalized their plans over the past two hours, while waiting for the right moment to arrive. Now Kincaid knew it had come.

'Let's go,' he growled, and stepped down into the street with fingertips brushing six-gun handle. This was his moment of truth, and suddenly with the stage set and the whiskey really kicking in, Kincaid felt ready to seize it with both hands. Eager. He believed nothing could halt them now.

He was also convinced that regardless of the sheriff's reputation, his partner, Cody, was unbeatable with a Colt .45 any place and must come out on top in any confrontation.

Cody himself was ice-cold calm as they proceeded across Main. Throughout the evening he'd been building himself up to this and could feel the lightning in his hands and a sureness rippling through him from head to toe. He'd never reckoned the lawman his better and was ready to prove it.

Ashton was berating Martin's sidekick, Hogue, as the two men approached.

'Get mounted and get out of town, Hogue,' he stated flatly. 'You are posted for two weeks and—'

'Leave that boy be, Ashton!'

Cord swung to face the challenge, eyes widening fractionally when he saw Kincaid and Cody. In back of them a crowd was already quickly beginning to gather in the street almost as though they'd been waiting for this. . . .

'Kincaid,' he said. 'What—?'

'Shut your mouth, I'm doing the talking, tinstar,' Kincaid snarled, bracing his legs and letting his hand hang close to gunbutt. 'What happened at the spread didn't finish anything between us – just got it started, is all. I've stood back and watched you swagger and strut your way around this town . . . while crawling about on your sneaky yellow guts after my sister. But that game's over. I'm giving you two choices, turn in that badge and be gone by daybreak . . . or go down!'

'The man is right, Cord,' Brett Cody supported. 'We've both had a gutful of you . . . this whole town has, by God. And if you think I'm going to sit back while you make a play for Barbara you've made your biggest mistake that could also be your last, tinstar!'

Cord stood motionless as the diatribe continued. Across the street another crowd was swelling and the tension building. This mob could plainly tell this wasn't simply Stirling Kincaid sounding off for show as he was prone to do at times. This was the real thing.

By now the whole town had learned of the fight and those who knew him best realized Kincaid's pride wouldn't let him endure the humiliation he was known to have suffered today.

And they were right.

Pride, rye whiskey and overriding vanity had brought Stirling Kincaid to this moment of truth. Ashton had humiliated him and shamed his family. There was but one way for a gentleman of honour to respond. His anger raged.

'Last chance, Ashton. Unbuckle that Colt and be gone by sunrise – or I'll kill you where you stand!'

The crowd was suddenly hushed, the sound of a baby crying somewhere sounding loud. With every eye fixed on him the sheriff stood staring his challenger down for what appeared to be an eternity.

Then abruptly he turned away!

'I'm not fighting you, Kincaid,' he said distinctly over his shoulder. 'I won't.'

And strode away with Kincaid's words ringing in his ears.

'You are a yellow dog, Ashton. You are a phoney and a fake and I was the one who always knew it!'

The sheriff of Sugar Creek kept walking.

CHAPTER 10

SILENT GROW THE GUNS

Three Twenty Mile cowboys galloped the full length of Federation Street firing off their guns into the night sky. They swung off at the Diamond Corral and came thundering back as Mayor Garroway and banker Jobe Calvin appeared hurrying along the plankwalk. A pane of glass in the wheelright's went out with a crash and ragged street youths howled with excitement as they rushed in to plunder the exposed treasures.

Exchanging harried glances the two council members hurried on, virtually the only respectable citizens to be seen upon the streets by this. The wide and dusty main avenue once again belonged to the miners and cowboys, the riff-raff, the drunken, the out-of-work and the just plain no account.

The hellraisers resembled unruly children with the schoolmaster absent, yet the same men were capable of turning violent at virtually any moment, something the citizens of Sugar Creek knew only too well from the bad old days before Ashton came to town.

Turning in at the American House the two councillors headed directly for the stairs. They had called by at the jailhouse twice in the past two hours looking for Ashton, but without success. The decision to search for him here was driven by a rising fear that the whole situation might be getting out of hand, slipping away.

They reached Ashton's door where Garroway raised a ham fist and hammered loudly.

'Sheriff Ashton, this is Garroway!'

No response.

'Please open up, Ashton,' Jobe Calvin urged. 'We must talk with you.'

There was only silence from Room 15, and after a minute the sounds of the visitors' footsteps fading back down the stairs was all there was to be heard, followed by stillness.

Seated in his shadowed room by the open windows with a cigar glowing in his hand, the sheriff of Sugar Creek nodded to himself. Whoever it had been, they were gone. He inhaled deeply and watched the stars shine down upon what felt like the longest night of his life.

He had broken his own iron rule. . . .

That was the dominant thought as he listened to the sounds of drunken revelry rising from below. For right from the outset of his career when he'd first pinned on a sheriff's star years ago he had understood that strong personal relationships were not for men like him. They only weakened you and made you vulnerable.

So, how come he had faltered?

He understood only too well. Deep down he understood the simple truth that a town-tamer was simply flesh and blood like everybody else. He had discovered this when he had fallen in love. This had exposed his vulnerability to his enemies and now they had taken full advantage.

Now the rock he'd built his life upon was cracked and before this night was through he might well see it crumble altogether.

'No!'

It was his own voice and it surprised him with its force. It was as though he'd been jolted from a trance as he stood and reached for gunbelt and hat.

He'd had his moment of human weakness and self-doubt but he was now the iron lawman again. And this was his town to save . . . or to perish in the attempt!

Within minutes he was back upon the street 'showing the gun' and keeping the lid on the trouble spots by the sheer force of his presence.

And so managed to maintain full authority – until

the big brawl erupted at the Prairie Flower.

Even before he got there a sixth sense told him it was a bad one, maybe that full-blown showdown he'd wanted to avert, yet would not walk away from should it erupt.

He'd walked away from here once, the time he quit the town. He'd vowed never to do so again, not even if confronted by a danger that might well prove the greatest he'd ever faced in his gunfighter's life.

He set off to prowl the half-wrecked and fear-jangled town until someone told him where she was. . . .

'Oh, Cord, Cord! Brett's been gunned down!' Barbara Kincaid cried, and rushed across the room to throw herself into his arms.

'It's all right, Barbara,' he murmured, his gaze taking in the turbulent scenes of violence and chaos where the long bar had stood. 'Everything is fine . . . I'm here with you now.'

The half-wrecked Prairie Flower Saloon hushed as the lawman motioned to Lon Green to take care of the girl, then made his way across to the bar.

He'd received a full account of the violence and rioting from Tab Merrill before reaching the trouble spot, and the reality proved as bad as he'd feared, maybe even worse.

A wild outbreak of unrestricted rioting and pillage while he was occupied at the opposite end of Federation Street had finally concentrated and exploded here at the biggest saloon in town where blood had spilled and where seemingly every big man with a stake in taking over this town – his town – had come together to stake his claim or exact revenge while the sheriff patrolled their streets elsewhere.

Bottles were still being hurled and there was the sound of weeping and groaning from wrecked corners and darkened passageways as the familiar upright figure strode into the chaos.

A reeling drunk emerged from the half shadows brandishing a Colt. Ashton drew and fired and the figure toppled, clutching a shoulder.

Cord swung to confront fully the scenes of carnage along with the faces of the fearful, the drunken, the hate-driven and the drugged-out – as well as those faces that met his stare without fear but with a primitive hatred a man could smell.

This was the night he'd known must come almost from the day he'd decided to return. Fate had designated it and wherever his eye fell it was met by suspicion, hatred, vengefulness and lethal intent.

For he had dominated these hard men, shot and jailed their friends, defying them every day with his sober solitariness and that damned black gun.

They had backed up, slunk away and drowned their hatred in whiskey and gin while waiting for . . . The Day!

And suddenly like a message from the dark gods it was here. Their day of courage and revenge – and he just one man alone!

He felt their hatred like a physical push but nothing showed in his face except an iron purpose which seemed enough over long moments to impress and cower even the most hate-driven and dangerous amongst them. He was back and was stronger than ever before as he propped amidst the chaos to face them down.

He didn't speak as he stared at the crumpled dead body of Brett Cody before switching his bleak gaze to Kincaid's bruised and glowering face, and finally, inevitably, turning to confont Wild Jack Mason.

Mason, of course, was the wild card in this deck. Ashton might have assessed the chaos he'd witnessed as simply a case of a half-tamed town kicking over the traces when the man committed to maintaining order – himself – had faltered . . . but for Mason.

He only had to stare across at the busted bar where the gunfighter leaned indolently on one elbow with a crooked smile to know that Mason had simply remained in exile while awaiting this moment when time and circumstance and the gods of the gun would lead him forth into the spotlight of his notoriety.

With McCrow already under the ground, Wild Jack stood alone and exalted by his violent minions. And if Death could walk and talk it might have looked and sounded just like him as he tilted his dark head back and spoke in that odd whispering voice.

'The good gambler always knows when to quit

before the cards turn against him, Ashton. Yet somehow I always knew you'd be too proud and too dumb to know when that day dawned for you!'

Maybe he should have anticipated this, Ashton mused as evil laughter rippled through the battered, smoke-clouded saloon. Yet he thrust the thought aside and accepted the reality; of a town gone loco; the wild ones in control; a dozen ways a man could die. But there was maybe one chance left . . . if only he had the nerve to ignore the swarm of rioters . . . and to risk all by striking directly for the uprising's deadly heart. . . .

He didn't speak loudly yet his words carried to every corner of that room.

'I will have your gun now, Jack.'

Mason reacted. 'My gun, lawdog? What is this? That was a fair fight.'

'Not between a man of your ability and Brett Cody, it wasn't. We had an agreement, and you broke it. Now you will hand me your gun and you will quit town.'

Twin spots of anger appeared high on the gunman's gaunt cheekbones as people began to edge away from the bar.

'I surrender my gun to no man, Ashton. Not to you. Not to anybody.'

'You'll give it or I'll take it.'

'No, Cord, no!' cried Barbara Kincaid, but was restrained by Lon Green's strong grip.

'You'll only bury yourself if you push me too far,

Ashton,' Mason warned, eyes like chips of blued steel. 'Like I say, I give my gun over to no man and that goes double for any yellow lawman.'

Ashton nodded soberly.

'Words won't do it, man. I won't back down to you, but I will have that gun.'

'Then go straight to hell!' Mason raged, and slashed at his hip.

Two hands sped down, two guns came hissing from holsters and muzzles spewed fire and leaden death.

Ashton ducked as Wild Jack's slug clipped his shell belt causing one bullet to explode and keyhole through the floorboards between Stirling Kincaid's boots. Next instant, Mason began staggering towards the doors and those closest to the gunman saw the ugly dark stain on his shirt at the back where the sheriff's slug, ripping clear through the body, had come out.

Lurching drunkenly through roiling clouds of billowing gunsmoke, Wild Jack Mason fired again, the bullet tugging at Ashton's shirtsleeve. He triggered back twice and Mason was sent tumbling, clutching desperately at nothing, dead before the floorboards hit his face.

Unscathed and grimly calm, Cord Ashton stepped back from the man he had just killed, then abruptly ducked and spun as a revolver churned close by, sending lead screaming over his shoulder.

'Stirling – no!' screamed Barbara, as her brother,

his face a twisted mask of savagery and with a smoke-belching gun in his hand, made to trigger again.

But there was no stopping Stirling Kincaid. For in his obsession, the man who had provoked the riot and subsequently inflamed a town gone crazy had convinced himself that when the dust finally settled Ashton would be disgraced, and the power would be his own to assume what he had always craved, which was complete control. To this end he'd brought in Wild Jack and his henchmen and had been ready to celebrate his triumph when in the space of mere minutes Ashton had reappeared to loom taller than ever with Wild Jack lying dead at his feet.

Kincaid's eyes went insane with fury, and he swung his smoking cutter upon Ashton, who was backing away and making no move to raise his Colt.

He could not kill her brother.

The Prairie Flower rocked once again to the detonating blast of a six-gun and a gaping mob saw Cord Ashton stagger from the impact. The shot had been intended to kill but Kincaid was so shaken by rage his bullet had merely clipped Cord's shoulder.

Yet still Ashton made no move to retaliate. And clutching his weapon with both hands now Kincaid lunged towards him, roaring in triumph.

A gun thundered but no bullet found the lawman. Instead Stirling Kincaid reeled as if struck by a giant fist, sending him spinning slowly around to see the smoking cutter in a white-faced Lon Green's right hand.

'Drop it, Stirling!' Green yelled.

His back against the wall with blood trickling from shoulder and side, Cord Ashton saw Kincaid's gun level on the youth, and only now, with both Lon and Barbara both in imminent danger, did he bring his own gun sweeping upwards again.

Yet he never fired as Lon Green, unflinching and resolute, levelled his weapon and calmly triggered twice. Stirling Kincaid's powerful body jerked convulsively and he reeled backwards with arms outflung, blood spilling from his gaping mouth.

And fell, never to move again.

Ashton did not look at Kincaid. Nor did he look at Lon Green's face, so pale and ashen now as he slowly lowered that smoking gun. Instead he watched only Barbara, waiting for the hate he expected to see leap to her eyes, dreading it and knowing it would wound him worse than a bullet ever could.

Yet that which he dreaded did not come to pass as in the shocked silence Barbara took two uncertain steps towards her dead brother then halted to turn slowly towards Ashton. Then she rushed to him with tears flooding her eyes and her hands going up to his face. 'Oh, Cord, are you all right?'

His gun thudded to the floor and he held her to himself fiercely. 'I'm all right, Barbara,' he whispered against her hair. 'Now. . . .'

The afternoon was green and gold with spring. The rainy season was past and underneath the heavy branches of the oaks where Barbara Kincaid stood with Cord Ashton gazing down upon her brother's grave, the grass grew green and sweet all around.

Out across the Silver Dollar's rolling hills the feed was lush and thick. Sagebrushes shone with new silver leaves and cottonwoods were clothed in rich green. Fat cattle dotted the slopes and down past the fence surrounding the little graveyard where Lon Green sat on the railing by the horses, two clumsy young calves were butting their heads together, drawing back then butting again.

It was a Sunday, weeks since the tumultuous events in Sugar Creek, and Ashton's first day abroad. His right arm was still in a sling but the pain was fading every day, much like the memory of that bloody night.

'It is so calm here, Cord,' the girl murmured as they finally turned away to climb to the crown of the hill and gaze out over the vast sweep of the Silver Dollar. 'Do you believe Stirling would be at peace now?'

'Resting here at Silver Dollar? Yes, I reckon so, Barbara. For he really loved this place. He might have been wrong in other ways but nothing could change the way he felt about the land. I've thought about things like that a lot lately and no matter how you look at events, your brother did most of what he did for love of the ranch.'

'I know it, Sam. His downfall was his obsessive fear of dying without an heir. Yet ironically, that is exactly what happened.' Her eyes searched his face. 'I wonder if there might ever be an heir to the Silver Dollar, Cord?'

'Why, I guess that's largely up to you, Barbara. For that depends on whether you will marry me or not.'

The girl's eyes snapped wide. 'What did you just say, Cord Ashton?'

He slipped his arms about her waist. 'I've had time to do a lot of thinking and I realized the time can come when a man has tamed enough tough towns and taken enough foolish chances, and it is time to put down roots. Ramrod Valley is still wild but in time it won't need a lawman with a gun. I could see myself doing less and less on the streets and more and more out here working the land . . . that is, if someone wanted me to?'

His response was in her kiss and tears rolled down her cheeks. 'Oh, Cord, it's made me happier than I can say to hear you speak that way. But do you really believe the town could ever be so peaceful you could hand over to somebody else?'

'I surely do,' he said with a sly smile. 'Matter of fact, I've already got in mind the very man who I could train to take over all those responsibilities.'

'But . . . but where on earth would you find somebody like that so soon. . . ?'

He smiled and turned, indicating the distant figure sitting upon the corral fence. 'Somebody who has already proven up to the job even if he is still a boy.'

'Lon – why, of course. Have you mentioned it to him, Cord?'

'Not yet.'

She squeezed his hand. 'Then let's go ask him. And while we're at it . . . we can tell him about us.'

Cord Ashton smiled, and hand in hand they walked through the sunlight down the green slopes to where Lon Green was waiting.